There Is No Year

About the Author

Blake Butler is the author of the novella *Ever* and the novel-in-stories *Scorch Atlas*, named Novel of the Year by *3:AM Magazine*. He edits *HTMLGiant*, "the internet literature magazine blog of the future," as well as two journals of innovative text, *Lamination Colony* and *No Colony*. His writing has appeared widely online and in print, including in *The Believer, Unsaid, Fence,* and *Vice,* and short-listed in *The Best American Nonrequired Reading.* Butler lives in Atlanta and blogs at gillesdeleuzecommittedsuicideandsowilldrphil.com.

Also by Blake Butler

Scorch Atlas

Ever

HARPER ● PERENNIAL

NEW YORK ● LONDON ● TORONTO ● SYDNEY ● NEW DELHI ● AUCKLAND

author of Scorch Atlas

Blake Butler

There Is No Year

a novel

HARPER ● PERENNIAL

HarperCollins books may be purchased for educational, business, or sales promotional use. For information please write: Special Markets Department, HarperCollins Publishers, 10 East 53rd Street, New York, NY 10022.

FIRST EDITION

Title page photograph by Milan Bozic

All other photographs by Justin Dodd

Designed by Justin Dodd

Library of Congress Cataloging-in-Publication Data is available upon request.

ISBN 978-0-06-199742-6

11 12 13 14 15   OV/RRD   10 9 8 7 6 5 4 3 2 1

For no one

For years the air above the earth had begun sagging, suffused by a nameless, ageless eye of light. This light had swelled above the buildings. It caked on any object underneath.

This light, unlike most other light, outside itself could not be seen, could not be felt impressed upon each inch of air and body. It had no length, no temperature, no speed.

Each day the light grew gently thicker, purer. Each day still felt the same. Its presence rode in ridges on the faces of the hours and in silent hair all down all arms.

At night the light would be called dark. Among the dark the people staggered, aligned upon the air with hidden halls. In hidden halls they bumped and built their homes.

Each of these homes, no matter how small, held at least several outlets, doors, and bulbs. In each home, as well, several people, each fit with further holes inside them too.

Through these holes the light could enter, thereby: *naming*, thereby: *age*. Inside the light and homes the people made more people. The light, unlike the people, went on and on.

ONE

Those who live, live off the dead.
ANTONIN ARTAUD

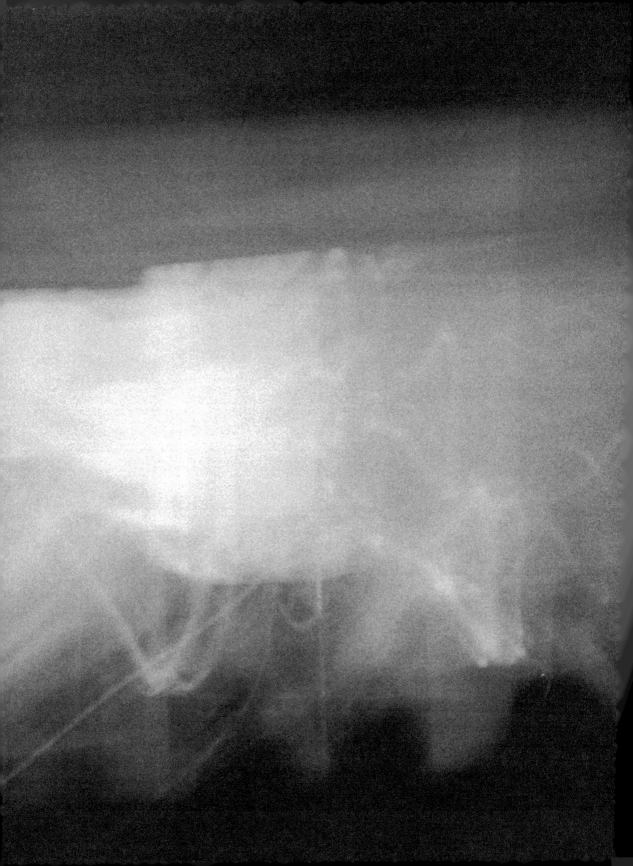

CONTROLLER

The father and the mother sat close together without touching. They weren't sure which way to aim their heads. They remembered recent rooms from other buildings. The house still felt so new.

They'd been sitting on the sofa for a long time. Neither felt sure just how long. They'd come downstairs to watch a movie—both with a certain one in mind—something they'd each seen once, somewhere, though not together. Now they could not remember.

The father felt too warm in this small room. He put his left arm around the mother, felt uncomfortable, took it back. He tried resting the arm on his knee or on his belly—still not right.

What if he could remove the arm, the father wondered? If he could remove the arm, he'd do it. This was the arm the father used most often to take his son or wife at certain soft times by his or her own arm, or other times to masturbate himself or eat.

The mother wrung her hands and flexed her neck and saw the ceiling. *There was something about the ceiling.* She hummed a song—a certain song—she thought she was making it up but she wasn't.

The father stood up.

The father sat down.

The father picked up the controller for the TV. He held it parallel to the floor. He turned to a channel that came in slanted. He turned to a channel that was not there. He mashed many other buttons, angry. The buttons' digits formed a certain sequence. The father turned the remote toward his head.

He pressed *OFF*. He pressed *OFF*. He pressed *ON*. He pressed *OFF*. He pressed *MUTE*. He pressed *OFF*. He pressed *OFF*.

ESTATE

The father had bought the house with paper money. He'd worked for years and years. If asked he could not say for certain what the work was. Mostly all he did all day any day was look into a blank screen flush with light. Sometimes the father looked at porn or ads or sports scores, but mostly just the light.

In the nights before the new house, the father walked up streets peeping through glass. He'd seen the light in other houses. He'd seen people in their beds—sometimes moving in the darkness to the bathroom or the stairs. He'd seen so many bodies fuck. In one house he'd seen someone reading about a father at the window in a book. All the houses touched by wire. The grain in the glass in the windows in the frames in the walls in the rooms in the houses on the yards along the streets aligned for miles.

The father wanted a certain kind of life to give his family. He wanted a house described by all of who he'd been—though who he'd been, to him, would not stop changing.

The father washed and washed his hair. He tried. He concentrated.

He had not asked the mother or son what she or he thought before he signed the family name on legal lines. He could not remember where he'd found the listing. He could not remember what he did not remember—nor would he want to, would he ever.

There were many things the father did without his wife's permission—things like seeing, walking, aging—things he could not name.

From outside the new house looked like many other houses.

COPY FAMILY

When the family came to live inside the new house, they'd found another family already there. An exact copy of their family—a copy father, mother, and son. The copy family members stood each in a room alone unblinking. The copy family would not speak when spoken into—though they had heartbeats, they were breathing. Their copy eyes were wet and stretched with strain. Their copy skin felt like our skin. Their copy hearts beat at their chests.

The father flicked the copy father on the arm there by the window in the kitchen—the window where on so many coming days the father would look out onto the yard—the yard where once the copy family had surely moved and laughed and dug and thought and fought and seen the sky change color. The father watched the copy father flinch. The copy father's big ring finger had thirteen copy rings on. In the copy father's copy eyes the father could read his other's current scrolling copy thoughts:

This is my house.

This is our house.

This is where I am.

WHAT ELSE COULD THEY HAVE DONE?

The family took the copy family and they set them on the back porch. The father carried the copy father and the mother the copy mother and the son his. The skins of the two families smushed together grunting. Their sweat became commingled. The copy family members did not wink or speak or cause commotion. They did not jostle in their stance.

The only thing that made the family different from the copy family was instead of teeth the copy family's mouths were lined with mold. As well, the copy son appeared exhausted, sticky. He had dark meat around his eyes. The copy family's breath came out cold and made no sound.

The son wanted to play dress up with his copy body but the father smacked the son across the head. The father hated when his son played girl games. The father bought the son a new neon football for Christmas and his birthday every year. The father also bought the son a

football on the father's birthday, a form of begging. Sometimes he found he could convince the son to come out into the yard, though no matter how soft the father threw the ball or how close they stood together, the son could never catch. Even right there. Even touching.

The son's hands and fingers always itched. Sometimes the itching spread into his knee. Sometimes the only thing about the son at all was all the itching. The son was older than he looked.

PRETEND TO NOT BE THERE

In the new house wrung with coarse light, the father locked the doors and sealed the eaves. He had the family play Pretend To Not Be There. They waited to see if the copy family would simply disappear or go away. They waited several hours, peeping. Later, they hooted and shook their arms, made fire. The copy family would not retort.

The mother found the copy family's TV dinners in the freezer and off the floor the family ate: defrosted veggie medley, veal cordon bleu. There was even a little cheesecake wrapped in black plastic. The family felt run through. They felt their bodies rumble, squealing. The copy family outside in the night. The father, mother, and son each with one wall between them and their copies, eating.

The father sent the son to bed. He and the mother went with the son into the certain room they'd let the son himself select—he could have had many other rooms. The bed was deep

and clean and padded. The parents took turns kissing the son on the brow, the wrists, the thumbs, the mouth, the teeth, the back, the stomach. The son went right to sleep. Just after, in the hallway, the father touched his hand against his lips, feeling for the cells that'd come off in transference—what parts of himself he'd left upon the son.

THE COPY MOTHER, IN PARTICULAR

The father and the mother stayed up well into the evening watching the copy family stand. The father and the mother agreed they had to do something—*something*—*what?* They could not go on like this, even a little. The copy family had not moved an inch. They could call police but what would happen? Light from the backyard's sensor-triggered flood lamps clicked on and off without clear provocation.

The copy family would not go away. The father worked himself into a state, shouting curse words, splaying arms. He went out to the car and got a softball bat he'd used for pickup games in college—he'd not once had a hit, though he'd been beaned more times than he could count on all the hands in all the houses on the street where his house stood—he could often still remember how the ball felt each time, banging fast into his muscle—how his chest would scrunch and then expand—how he sometimes seemed not there at all. The father stood at the window with the weapon. He threatened legal action. He spoke in un-

intended rhyme. He said his own name to the copy father. The copy father seemed to have more hair than him.

By the time the morning came on gnawing, the father had collapsed. He lay fetal-curled on the laminated kitchen floor, his back against the fridge door, shook. The mother stood over the father. The mother took the softball bat away. She smoothed a blanket over her husband. She covered up his head. She turned on the radio in the intercom that'd been wired to broadcast through the house. There wasn't music, but people talking—many people all at once. She turned the volume louder. The speech sound filled the house—filled in on the air around their breathing bodies.

The mother clasped her hands. She went out on the porch and stood among the copy family, silent.

There she was.

SMOTHERING, THE MOTHER'S KNOWLEDGE OF

In the copy mother's copy face the mother saw the way the years had run her down—the slow stretched lines of older versions sunk to layers—the cheekbones taut and caked with rouge. The mother hulked her copy body off the ground. She carried her copy body in the weird light strumming downward off the shifting sky in sheets. The mother moved through the crunched grass to the concrete to the swimming pool the house had come with. Her copy body hummed hot and burbled. She held herself the way she'd hold a massive baby. She threw her copy body out into the pocket of caught water, watched her splash down, watched it burp. The copy mother did not struggle. The pool was green with straw and algae and old rain. The mother could not see the bottom. The water stunk. A string of silent glassy bubbles rung up from the copy mother's copy head. Her body sunk into the muck and did not rise. Along the top the mother watched a scrim of pollen slosh in waves. The windows of the house next door were all cracked open and opaque. The house next door to that house did not have doors or windows, walls at all.

CLOSER

The mother found the copy father's skin felt rather pleasant—softer than her husband's—responsive to her touch. She spread her fingers in the soft short hair over his forearm. She whispered in his ear. She said the things she'd meant to say.

She closed the copy father's eyes.

When the copy father's body hit the water, his shirt and pants soaked darker several shades. The copy father's skin became distended. The water boiled. The copy father's copy body tried a while to stay floating on the pool's surface in the muck but the mother pushed it down. She held it under with her foot and then the pool net. She ran a tongue across her teeth. The moon hung over the backyard had a sliver missing from its center. All the homes held underneath that light.

Suddenly the mother felt a voracious thirst for pork.

16

THE COPY SON, IN PARTICULAR

The mother returned from what she'd done then to stand above the copy of her son. There was very little about his copy body that betrayed any major difference from its other—in fact, if the mother hadn't known for sure already her true son was upstairs curled in the new bed the father and the mother had bought him—*no more nits yet in the mattress, nothing eating where he slept*—if she wasn't sure for sure the true version of her boy was up there with his sleep eyes spinning in his head—*wasn't he?*—if she hadn't put him there herself—she wasn't sure that she could tell him from this child here—this child with the same scar along his forearm like the one the son had gotten fallen fainting from a tree—he was not supposed to have been walking yet—he'd been bedridden for so long—*trying to reach the sun, he'd explained later.* This child here had the same black pockmarks where disease had come into the son's body, searching his flesh for what it wanted—*when the son had stayed alive the doctors seemed more nervous than relieved—how peculiar, they kept saying, it's against science.* This child here had the same blond bowl-cut hair like the son, hair the mother could barely bring herself to snip, every inch of him her precious—*such nights she'd*

dreamed of his insides, swimming deep inside his cells. This child, this boy—he was made of her, and she was made of him.

No, the mother could not bring herself again to do the thing she'd done twice just now already.

No.

NO

The mother peeped through the window from the outside to make sure her husband was still sleeping. Under the blanket, she watched him wriggle. The father had always been a rowdy sleeper. Most nights he kept the mother up straight through till morning. The mother slept most during the day, if ever. The sleeping father spoke in languages the mother had not heard—*if she'd heard them she could not remember.* The sleeping father chewed the skin inside his mouth to bits.

In a hurry, slunk and brooding, knowing what the father, waking, might have to say, the mother fire-lifted her son's copy body on her shoulder and carried him silent through the night. She moved into the thick lip of trees grown up and out around the house, into which no fake light showed. She carried the body through the thick murk, keeping careful not to fall. The earth around was eaten up with tunnel. There was wobble. There was grease. There were creatures out here somewhere. She could hear their tiny teeth. There were

holes in the soil that led to somewhere. The mother moved by feel. The mother carried her son's copy body through the forest through a tunnel lined with crud. Through the tunnel came a clearing. Set in the clearing there was wire. The wire scorched the mother's hand. Still she knew what she was seeking. She knew that she would know.

When she arrived in or at some small exact place, the mother set the copy son's soft copy body down. In the mud, the light around his copy body began bending—the mother basking briefly in that fold—the son set underneath her old and getting older, his copy skin turned mirrored, bright. The son's holes among the bending gave off a thick dark smoke— smoke rose in burst toward the sky—it rushed in rising as if to bend that surface also, *wanting*, only soon to disappear there somewhere high above, the tendrils birthed and blown away to unseen, sunken—diffused though holes in holes in holes—rips the sky had hidden in its years on years and days on days. The copy child and mother went on still there beneath it, frying, one breath fed back and forth between. They purred secret sentences in silent rising spiral until the sky at last had drunk so much it sunk to night—*the night not out of cycle but in insistence, demanded in the skin*, the unseen smoke of body after body sewn surrounding until the mother, at least, could not see—could not feel the air even around her, or her other—could not feel anything at all—and in the dark the mother stuttered— and in the dark again the mother walked.

A GOOD DAY

The next day there was nothing wrong. No one was coughing. There were no bills. The sun rose in the morning and felt warm and not oppressive. The yard looked bright and clean. The mother made the son breakfast and drove him to where he was supposed to be and she came home alone and felt okay. The father called her twice to ask how she was without any preamble of suspicion.

The mother made herself an egg sandwich and found just enough hot sauce in the bottle to make it tasty, eliminating the chance that she might overdo it and make the eggs too saucy and thus inedible, as she had a tendency to do. She solved the newspaper's word puzzle in record time without even really understanding how she knew the answers.

The father's stocks went up enough to alleviate a recent downswing since they'd moved into the house. The father sat in his office with his stock tracker open, watching the num-

bers replace one another on the screen. He masturbated in the handicapped stall without any other person coming in. His size felt fine.

At school the son made a friend. A new girl in town from out of town. The girl resembled the son in many features—*skin, lips, cheeks, hair, teeth, build, height, sound*—but because she was female he did not notice. The girl was very rude to teachers, but in a way the son found wise. The girl wore long black gloves. The girl had two different colored eyes, one of which would be looking at the son and the other eye of which seemed to toggle. She would not tell the son her proper name. She had a lot of nicknames she liked for him to say aloud. The girl ate with her mouth open and the food all falling out.

The son enjoyed the girl. He felt happy to have a friend.

When the family got home, all at the same time, they gathered around the kitchen table and played Monopoly. They all landed on FREE PARKING every other time around. Everyone was able to buy the properties that they needed, and the bank ran out of money, and the game ended in a tie. Afterward the son did a stand-up routine he'd written at school from a deep sleep. The parents were impressed by the breadth and maturity of his jokes. They couldn't stop laughing—it made their heads ache, it was all so funny. Even when the son cursed the parents didn't mind because it added. Our child is . . . child is . . . entertaining! one parent told the other, fighting for breathing, though later they could not remember which had said and which had heard.

For dinner they ordered pizza and it arrived a little late and the pizza guy refused to take their money though he did accept a small tip and the pizza was still warm and even more delicious since they'd had that extra time to let their stomachs think. Instead of TV or closing themselves in their individual rooms the way most nights went, they sat around the

table long after dinner and talked about things that made them glad or things they wanted to become in the future or things about themselves and one another that they liked. They found themselves saying things that they wanted, things they did not know they wanted— *the mother candles, the son a black pen, the father a new pair of working gloves*—and therefore felt the bloom of some new direction.

They went to bed together, all at once, without discussing, and they didn't feel the need to lock their doors. They fell asleep quickly without thinking and their dreams were full of bliss or magic, some kind of wondrous unfamiliar which in the coming days of daylight would itch and itch against their lives.

ROOM OF HAIR

The father spent coming weekends painting over the walls of several rooms. At move-in the house's walls had been all a shade of blue so blue it appeared black. In certain rooms the walls had been augmented with intricate designs and tiny lines of texts, though these as well were rendered in the same blue and thus could not be seen. The paint the father swathed over the old paint hid the old paint from the eye. The father's body groaned with all his reaching. The wall's length often seemed to grow. The father would paint and paint and paint and still have hardly painted anything at all.

In the evenings now before his sleeping the father walked for hours through the house— room to room to room there, seeing. The house seemed larger than it was. Many rooms were long and had no windows. Firetraps, they might be called. Other rooms had shelves or holes or seating built right into the body of the house. Doors with odd knobs. Patterned carpet. Bulbs in certain lamps he'd need would burst. Sometimes the father liked to leave

the lights off from one room to another, fumbling for something, bumping his shoulder or kneecap on something hidden, hard. At doorways he would flick the light on half a second, burst the room bright, then in the returning dark try to negotiate the space by mirror in his mind. In certain rooms the father found it hard at all to breathe.

One room on the second floor had a dumbwaiter which would whine along its string, and when pulled rose to somewhere overhead, straight up. There was nothing above the second floor as far as the father knew, except the roof, the sky, the light. One night the father placed an empty water glass into the dumbwaiter. He closed the small door and pulled the pulley. He waited long enough to smoke a cigarette then he brought the box back down. The glass had been turned on its side. The rim felt wet. The father put an orange inside and brought it up and brought it down and found the orange had lost its color. The father wrote a note on a piece of paper—WHO IS IN THERE—and brought it up and brought it down and found the paper rendered blank. The father was too large to fit into the dumbwaiter himself. The father bought a padlock.

Off the house's longest hallway, the father found a room the realtor had not shown the father—a room also not on the father's copy of the blueprints, a room so small the father could hardly fit inside—this room was stuffed with hair. Wispy black hair, the kind a cat sheds, though it didn't smell like cat. The father found himself pressing his head into the hair, breathing, breathing. The father had been balding steadily for at least the past two years. All the other men in the father's family kept their hair. In fact, the father's father had grown his hair beyond his ass—enough hair to wrap the father's father's body before they'd buried him at sea.

Nestled in the hair against the seamless wooden floorboards, the father found a key. The key seemed wider than most locks. The father clenched the key inside his fat fist. The father

swallowed something in him. The father closed the tiny room. The father walked the key into the kitchen and placed it in a drawer with all the steak knives. The father stood in the kitchen for an hour. The father went back to the tiny room. The father gathered all the black hair into a black trash bag and walked it outside to the street. The father went inside watched it through the window.

The father drank a beer. The father drank a beer.

DISEASE RELICS

The father came into a room and saw the mother standing silent with her fingers in her ears. The mother's long fake neon nails made the plugging mostly ineffective, but still the mother would not answer. The mother's eyes were open but she would not look directly at the father. She kept turning more and more away.

The room was full of stuff they'd had to stop using as a precaution of the son's disease. They were supposed to have thrown it out. Burned it. Burned the ashes. Buried the ashes' ashes in a sealed jar. Razed the land the jar was put in. Razed their minds of *if* and *else*. No one had come to make sure that these things happened, and so they had not happened. Instead the mother hid these things away. They were supposed to have gotten rid of his newly huge pajamas, his crusty sheets, his loose hair and teeth—*the teeth he would have lost eventually anyway and the teeth he should have worn forever*—his unopened Study Bible and his tooth-

brush and his lost teeth, the baby book the mother had used to transcribe the details of his birth and youth, as well as any photographs taken of him during the period and any cards or other mail that bore his name.

They were supposed to change his name. They were supposed to forget everything the son had said aloud up to that point. The father, at least, had done the last of these. Over afternoons he had collected and removed what he could find of the son's scribbling on reams of paper, the paragraphs in illegible legends, letters smaller than the eye hole of a pin, drawings of mazes, maps, and bodies, cribbed in among the glyphs of language, enough to fill a book. The father had as well thrown out any books he'd seen the son touch or look at or had heard read aloud by the mother's mouth. Any music. Any gist.

This son, the father sometimes heard himself say inside him, in someone else's voice, *should no longer be alive.*

In the room the mother stood wearing the white mask, holding the precautionary plaster cast she'd made of the son's chest—already crumbling—against her own chest, humming one long sound.

The father had tried to convince the mother that it was best to get rid of these things as they could hold the sickness in their fibers, but whenever he brought it up like that the mother would get down on her knees and scream and scream until he said okay.

Eventually the father had even begun to want them for himself. He did not tell the mother how for weeks he'd slept with a long lock of the child's hair until he'd woke and found he'd eaten it.

The father took the plaster molding from the mother and sat it on the carpet and unplugged the mother's ears and clasped her hands and squeezed. He put his mouth against her head.

Do you want to go to McDonald's? he said. Do you want to go to Chili's? Do you want to go to Outback? Do you want to go to Miami Subs Grill? Do you want to go to the Container Store? Do you want to go to Sharper Image? Do you want to go to Hooters? Do you want to go to Chi-chi's? Wait, Chi-chi's is out of business. Do you want to go to Kenny Rogers Roasters? Do you want to go to Denny's? Do you want to go to Great Clips? Do you want to go to Taco Bell?

The father did not know what had made him talk like that.

The father could not laugh.

HOW THE SON GOT SICK

For years the son believed the father when the father said he owned a live man's head—though years later, in the telling, the father swore he'd said *nothing of the kind*. The father told the son he kept the head locked in the attic in a safe in their old house. He said he'd bought the head from a woman on the street—a woman with wrinkled, thumbless hands and a mustache. The father claimed the head particular in its eating. The head liked ranch dressing on fruit salad. The head liked mayo by itself. The father told the son not to try to see the head because the head would bite the son. The father said the head had mentioned the son in particular as a thing he meant to eat.

The son went on for years and years with the head inside his head. He began to learn other things about it. He and the head had long talks and walked in sunsets. The head told him things about money and pornography and chess and investing and wilderness survival. The son was three years old at the beginning, and the head was there still when he was

nine. All through those years the son tried to guess the safe's combination with no luck, though his dry mouth spoke the numbers in the night.

The son's tenth birthday morning bore one condition: **go**. And so he'd gone. The son had gotten out of bed, sweated sopping wet with eyes not open, and walked downstairs and left the house. He walked straight on into the forest. He was thinking anything at all. He came to a small, hardwood gazebo. The gazebo was black and had words emblazoned, *long words*, *names on names*. A beehive hung from a cord in the gazebo's ceiling's center. In the son's hands he found a stick. With the stick he beat the hive down with wide swinging, expecting to be stung—stung and stung and swollen up all over, growing several times himself—*the son had thoughts inside his head*. Instead, the hive hit the ground in silence, the bees all stunned in seasoned sleep—a queen among them, held a god.

The son felt cheated. The son winged rocks. He shouted sick words into the hive's holes. He heaved the hive into the air over and over and watched it hit the ground. No matter what it was the son did the son could not get the bees to buzz up, to surround him, though on his tenth toss, the hive fell open. Inside the hive was chock with mazy tunnel. Something oozing, some white brine, a sound.

Cut in the wax there, runned with honey, the son saw the combination.

KEYS

In the morning, crushed with a warm air, the mother could not think of where to hide. She'd been left alone in the house again, like every other day—the father working, son at school. Usually the mother liked to be alone, swum in the peace. Sometimes she took her clothes off and went out into the backyard and stood and sang and walked around, performing common household habits like any other except with her boobs and ass hung in the sun, as she had when she was teenaged on strange beaches on vacation from her childhood house. The mother felt young out in the wrecked light naked. The mother could spend years inside those days.

Today the mother's spit was brown like coffee. She ground her teeth, felt them diminish. She could not shake the sense of someone there behind her. She kept feeling something brush against her back. In all the rooms the curtains seemed to rustle even when the a/c had been turned off. She'd been finding keys all around the house. She'd found a key in the

baking powder. She'd found a key taped to the window. A key inside a certain book on a certain shelf. A key tied into her hair. All the keys unlocked the house, though some had no teeth. The mother hid the keys in certain places. Still she kept hearing the front door open. She heard something moving on the roof.

She tried to hide in the hallway closet but something kept rustling in the towels. She tried to hide in the washing machine but it kept turning itself on. Even when she stood and watched the room in a long mirror she knew things happened every time she blinked her eyes.

Cramped up under the son's small bed, the mother found a purple folder full of photos of women ripped from magazines. Naked women—glossed and healthy—each much older than the son—their bodies seemed so clean. The son had adorned the women's heads with extra eyes and horns and speech bubbles saying awful things—text that went on and on for pages, cramped tight to dark black—*text that should have been destroyed*. In many of the drawings, a smaller version of the son crawled on or in the women. The mother replaced the photos as if she had not seen them. The mother went into her room and drew a cold bath, watched it wait.

HEADS

The family sat around a table. The father sat at the table's head looking straight ahead at no one. Behind the father's head there was a photograph of another man's head, hairy. The man seemed to stare into the father. The father had not noticed this picture. The mother had taken the picture without asking, and hung it without asking, and if asked she would not be able to say when or where it was shot or whom it pictured. The only person at the table who knew whom the picture pictured was the son, though he would never look at the picture long enough to see.

The table was filled end to end with food. There was so much food on the table that there wasn't any room for plates. The family picked the things they wanted out of the serving dishes, some of which were larger than their chests: pink meats and bruised fruit, slaws and sauces, all soft enough to eat without the teeth, pervaded by a common smell. No one knew who cooked the food. The father assumed it was the mother. The mother assumed it

was someone else. The son didn't think about it—he was already saying his own prayer in his head. The mother and the father waited for someone to say grace. They'd been saying grace for years together though they could not remember who mostly said it for them. They each kept waiting for one another to begin. Each time the father thought to speak up he'd feel like the mother was about to speak herself and so he'd stop and wait and then she wouldn't. Under the table, the father rubbed his crotch seam with his thumb. He ate.

They ate. They were so hungry. There were all these hours. They chewed and chewed and then they swallowed. The food moved into the family through the flesh made from older food.

Some dishes were so hot no one could stand them. The son used his ring finger as a ladle and got scalded. The mark resembled the impression of a missing, inch-thick wedding band. The son sucked the finger with one side of his mouth and stuffed cooler food in on the other. He did not want to slow down in fear he might not get enough of something.

ANOTHER ROOM ON THE SAME EVENING

In another room, a room without the family, an indentation grew into one wall—a new pucker wide enough to fit a wire hanger, a pinky finger, something lean—a rip someone could breathe through—a hole for seeing out or seeing in. The home went on in this condition.

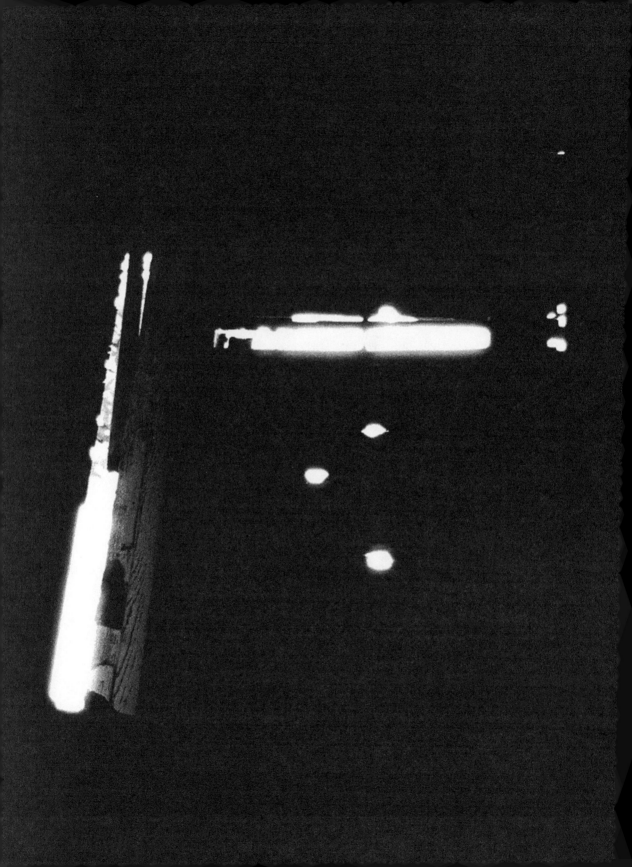

THE SKIN OF GOD

Outside, around the house, birds were landing on the roof. The birds could not stop shitting. The sun grew upon the white waste's sheen, showing the shrieking sky back at itself.

AFTER DINNER

The family all felt so stuffed they could not move. Though in their minds they were not full yet—had there been more food they would have ate and ate.

They had to crawl to the TV.

Usually the cable's crap connection delivered all the channels with a rind of fuzz. The screen would sometimes spurt and bubble with long rips of swish, often in the most important moments of a program, or at least the moments the person watching would most like to see. The cable company had sent several repairmen with no success. Several of the men had fallen off the roof, cracked bones or bruises. One of the men had lost his thumb.

That night the set kept changing channels.

They'd be watching *Trading Spaces* and the set would make a sound and the screen would blip to channel 48, a station that ran live feeds supplying info on local traffic and weather. Each time the blipping happened, the cameras seemed stuck above their very neighborhood, their street. There in the center of the screen they could see their little house with the blood red roof with the strange pattern and the mold.

They'd be watching reruns of *The $100,000 Pyramid* and the set would make a different kind of sound and the screen would blip to 99, an adult pay-per-view-style station which for some reason came in clear. The family could see the rhythm and the thumping. They could hear the lady squeal. The son sat with his head three feet from the screen. The mother did not turn away. She heard her eyes move in her head, like mice, the pupils widening and resizing under the insistencies and contortions of the replicating light.

The father turned the set off and sent them both to bed at 4:35 p.m.

AN INVESTIGATION

The father started in the corner behind the front door. From hands and knees to tiptoes he combed the walls' perimeter inch by inch. He took down the still-framed photos, dragged the TV stand, the bench. At the windows he felt for errors in the glass, anyplace where fingers or wire or some other form or fiber could slip in. He dumped the cushions off the sofa and pet the frame seams, looking for bumps or tears or places sewn up, anyplace something could have been hidden.

Every few minutes the father went to throw up again in the kitchen into a yellow trash bag over the sink. Each time he tied the sack and sat it nestled in another, building a tidy, plastic nest. His arms seemed muddy. Seeing made him weak. The father had been feeling sick for several days now—it got worse the more he moved inside the rooms. Most nights since moving in the father dreamt of his skin peeled off in leagues—a surface pale enough to write on, wide enough to wrap the house.

In the kitchen, bedrooms, and bathrooms, he followed a similar procedure, removing the linens from the closets and the foodstuffs from the cabinets, running his hands inside each blank space over the flat surfaces of its innards. He petted the carpet for slits or patches, the way he'd hid certain photos from his mother as a kid, *self-created creases in the house*. He squeezed seat cushions, upended desk drawers, took the sheets off of the guest bed. He dumped a whole box of cereal out into the trash can and sniffed the crumbs. There was a ring inside the Corn Flakes, the inserted surprise: a black ring, gleaming, his size. He put it on, with all the others—*his huge hands*. He poured a carton of orange juice into the sink and watched it drain slow. He tapped the mirrors in the bathroom for hollow sounds behind the reflection.

Each thing the father touched became new things.

The father had all night.

LATE LIST

In the silence left over after, the father went around the house and made a list:

—*Unknown long scratch mark under recliner*

—*New bubbles in glass of guest room bedside lamp*

—*Did fan always spin counterclockwise?*

—*Son's dolls in storage: more than a few are missing both eyes*

—*Garage bees*

—*Marks of insertion near top of wall in hallway. Larger than a pushpin? Who hangs
    things up that high?*

—*Handprints in the dust on top of the bookshelf by the mirror*

—*Initials and phone # in address book: RPT 515-3033. Who is this?*

—*Burn or other smudge marks on hallway baseboard, some kind of chewing*

—*Living room ceiling dripping what?*

When not writing, the father clenched the list inside his mouth to keep his hands free so he could rummage. He bit down so hard, not realizing, his teeth went through the paper, through his lip. The blood fed him gulping, warm as from a mother's nipple, brown.

PASSAGE

On his knees down at the air vent in the guest bedroom, the father clasped his hands. He pressed his flesh against the grate's face's metal tines—a mazemap pressed around his eyes. Through the gaps a lukewarm air blew, moist like raindamp, stunk like rice. The screws that held the grate in had no divots in their heads. The father could not pry them up using his fingers. A screwdriver chipped the paint, caused him to cut his right hand open with its end—more blood, from a new hole, though this blood smelled not the same—not like blood at all, but charcoal. The father sucked the squirt. He pushed and battered at the grating, bumping his fists, saying god's name, until after some unapparent pattern, the vent's face fell off in his hands. *Another pucker.* The drywall shedded ash. Somewhere upstairs he heard a brief instance of strange brass.

The father had never seen such a large hole. The vent's revealed mouth matched exactly with his shoulders' width. He stuck his head in, already sweating, his teeth tight in his

gums. The passage went along a long way straight before him before it turned quick at a right angle, toward the TV room and to the kitchen, thereafter blooming out to other rooms. The father felt a sudden want to sing into the warm hole, to fill the house with sound. He could not think of any songs.

With his shirt between him and the metal, the father forced himself in along the hole. He felt he'd gotten fatter. His flesh-bulged form fit to the rectangle. His feet and shoes dangled in the air in the guest bedroom and then, following his ass, became drawn in.

Where in the vent the roof had ridges, he felt his back's long black hairs becoming ripped out of their pores. It kind of hurt more than it should have. The passage seemed too small. Some goop of residue caked on the pipe's sides was rubbing off all on his pants and hands, his hair. He tried to stop and back out from already several feet deep. The air was blowing hotter, harder, at his body. Like someone breathing. Somewhere: babies. Mothers. Money. His hips seemed swelling. His thighs were meat. The vent's skin sucked in all around him. Nearer. Leaning. The father cursed and breathed the ripping air. He half-called for someone to come and help him. Half-called less loud. Whispered, Help.

Help! His crotch was sopping. The air was thick, and more so the further in. He knew he should not be crawling any further—*what if someone came along and screwed the vent's grate face back on behind him, moved a dresser to block its eye?* And yet, ahead, where the vent curved in an L out of his vision, the waiting metal shined. The seizing of his cells inside the terror made the father's teeth taste sharp—made his heartbeat lurch inside him, metabolizing. The air grew warmer, quicker, tighter, the deeper still into the house the father crawled, still with his mind inside him thinking, Help

Help

Help

Help

Help

Help

Help

48

DECISION

That night on their mattress, lying spines entwined and sleeping, the dusty father and itching mother agreed by grunt how it was time to sell the house.

HIS

The son received a package in the mail. The son had not ordered anything or been expecting gifts, nor could he think of anyone remaining who would give him gifts or want to. The son had not given his new address to anyone he could remember, or spoken it aloud into the air, though he may have written it on a free contest entry at a local food chain, which made him eligible to win a free week of gym training: *Shape the Self Inside Your Self*. He planned to exercise unbounded if he won. He would one day ripple in bright light.

When the son was younger, the mother's mother had often sent the son things for no good reason. At Christmas, the mother's mother sent the son special food that arrived already rotting—she did it every year. Once the mother's mother had sent a shrunken gown and a locket with a name inscribed—the mother's mother's name, not the son's. Folded between the locket's metal halves there was a picture of a man. The man had

black hair grown down over most of his face. He always seemed to be looking directly at the son. The son tried to wear the necklace despite the father's protest but he felt it choked him anyway. The son threw the necklace out a window. He'd found it several times sindce then: around the neck of his favorite doll; looped over the brass knob to the closet. Once he'd coughed it up. The son could no longer see or feel the necklace around his neck if he put it on.

This package was not likely from the mother's mother, as this year she was underground.

This package fit the exact shape of the mailbox. It was black and weighed more than it looked like it should, and yet the son could lift.

The son didn't think too much about it. He had his mind cluttered with other things, like how at school no one would come near him and how when he went into certain rooms he gave off smoke and how ceilings always seemed just above his head. Even the teachers went on calling him the wrong name—sometimes the mother's name, sometimes the mother's mother's. Sometimes the son's name came out as silence, just these moving lips. Other names they used could be found inscribed on plaques and trophies in the glass box at the front of the school, with photos of students left from long ago. They were mostly ugly. It was a very, very old school.

The son took the package out of the mailbox and carried it into the house under his arm. He went up to his room without speaking to anyone—to tell his mother how the new shoes they'd bought over the weekend were now melting in the soles. Even if the son had gone searching, even if he'd felt ecstatic with new bright news, the son would have found no one in the house. They'd all gone off somewhere, maybe. Or they were hiding. Or something else.

Had someone been around to see the son come in, perhaps, they might have stopped him, touched his hand. What's in that package, they might have said. Let's make it open. You are so young to receive mail. Instead the son went into her room and closed the door and locked it and turned around and set down the package and took off his clothes and faced the wall.

THE SON'S BOOK

The son was writing a book. The son did not realize he was writing the book because most of the time while he was writing he was asleep or not paying attention or in the mind-set of doing other things. Some nights the son would believe he was playing putt-putt in the backyard with the plastic golf set his father had bought to try to get him interested in sports, but the son was actually writing the book. The son would think he was languid in front of the television watching some kind of program about trucks or swords, designed to ensnare young boys' attention, but the son was actually writing the book. The son had also mistaken himself for eating dinner, painting pasta, laughing, and brushing his teeth while he was actually sitting in his closet with the door shut and his fingers typing into a very small computer he didn't know he had.

The computer's keyboard did not have markings. The light gushed from its screen so bright it would for hours make the son not see. He could not see the words he'd already written as he wrote them, not even inside him. Nothing. His eyes spun in his head.

The words he typed weren't words. Or, more so, the words had more words in them, collapsing, like flame laid into flame. The words inside the words kept the son from sleeping, even while sleeping.

While all awake, when the son tried to write, any pen refused to release ink. Any pencils he found inside the house would be unsharpened or would break their tips or bend. By the time the son had found something else to write with—rock on concrete, chocolate syrup, mud or blood—he could no longer hear the words inside him, and out came small other words instead: HELLO. HELLO. HELLO. HELLO. Sometimes he could not move his hands or arms or teeth or eyes at all.

BOOK

The son's book contained all things.

The son's book enmeshed the threads of all events or lights or hours that had ever happened or would happen, or were happening right now.

The son's book contained the sound of wing meat contained in birds once thought extinct, and that meat's aging, worn to none—

it contained a diagram of long forgotten burned or buried cities and how to enter through their last remaining eyes, how to stay there in that

belowground and, of new duration, live—

it contained sonogram photography of the man
who in coming years would invent the thing that ruined us all—

it contained every word
deleted from all other extant books, everything that every author had said aloud in rooms
with no one while writing what words did end up appearing in those books, as well as all
other possible combinations of words and new words those same characters could have
made—

it contained instructions on how to stand on the surface of a camel's eye—

it con-
tained an interminable glisten—an unbreakable lock—

56

it contained the missing seventh
and eighth sides of the Clash's *Sandinista!*, written by a presence never mentioned in the
band, which when played at a specific volume at a certain vector would invoke an unre-
membered form of light—and a song deleted from that missing album—lyrics deleted
from that song—code words deleted from that language—time—

it contained a sister for
the son to speak to in the evenings when the whole house was not awake, whom he would
let his darkest language into, black pictures writ on black—

it contained a killer recipe
for Apple Brown Betty, enabling mesmerism, enabling sight of new rooms set upon
rooms—

it contained electronic conversations between Richard Nixon and Aleister Crow-

ley, convening under new moonlight to discuss the initiation of the construction of a translucent ceiling over the United States, a silent, hieroglyph-inscribed dome, to watch the waking and the sleeping, to see and see—

it contained air that the reader, underwater, could truly breathe—

it contained how to erupt a mansion from a dot; and from a mansion, sores—from sores, pistons—from pistons, night—from night, a thing without a name—so on—

it contained combinations to every locker in a high school buried underground in the mud around the house where the son had been born, the lockers' insides padded with a gummy, tasteless residue, no stink, *and underneath that gunk, another combination knob*—

it contained a verbal adaptation of the film that would be considered the sequel to every film existing and film thereafter and film not found, *the paper white—*

it contained various ingestible flavors, scents, and textures, imaginary numbers, sentences that destroyed themselves in their own utterance—

a mirror—a wet—a gun—

a time spit—lumps—

computers—

life—

it contained full texts of endless novels trapped inside the perished brains of certain women and certain men, and in presences neither man nor woman but spread among the several, silent scourging brains—

it contained the last words of every major-league baseball player ever and the lengths of their longest hairs—

it contained directions on how to find your way into a room held offscreen in *The Wizard of Oz*, *The Wizard*, and *The Wiz*, and the films contained in those films, in no punch line, the frames therein unshot, unscened, unframed—

it contained containment—

it contained.

The son's book was all one sentence.

The son's book did not glow.

The son's book would one day be line-edited by a hair-covered man in a small office with no windows and no doors.

The son's book is forthcoming from Modbellor & Watt in 2118, when there is no one remaining who can see.

LAWNWORK

The man stood up above her. From in the sun he looked down. The mother could not make out the man's face, or what about it. As she stood up to look closer she felt her body brim with empty blood. Her head went swelling, dizzy. She put her hands into the blur for balance. She saw the man move as if to want to help her, but before they touched he stopped himself. The man's hands were very large, rings on each finger. Friction. The mother felt a minor wish that he'd come on—that he could want that—that he would ever. The mother crouched back near the ground.

The mother had become covered, somehow, in motor grease. She had it on her hands and neck and face and blouse and pant legs and on her shoes. She felt embarrassed. She'd filled the mower with gasoline and checked the oil and kissed the engine and still it wouldn't run. She'd ripped the cord until her arm hurt. She'd kicked and squawked and invoked god. The yard needed to look clean.

The man was saying something. He made motions with his hands. The mother had yet to meet the other people living on their street—to even see their faces—though in the mornings she noticed cars leaving and in the evening they came back. The mother didn't know why she couldn't make out what the man was saying. She saw his mouth, the hair around it—so much hair. She watched his lips move in small directions. The man's hands were colored darker than the whole rest of his skin.

The man knelt down beside her. The man had on a yellow dress shirt buttoned all the way up and no tie, the shirt's neck loose around his throat as if it'd been tugged at, itching. Long black gloves hid his forearms with silky sheen. His pants were deeply pleated, like theater curtains. The pants comprised a pattern, wavering in the repeat as would a wall of heat. The mother caught herself staring into the pants transfixed, as in the toning. The mother's head filled up again with liquid. The man grinned. He stood back up. He came back down. He licked his thumb and touched the mower. He was very near the mother.

With long, thick fingers, the man lifted the mower and peered into its mottled belly. He blew a silent breath into the engine, *a simple trick*. He stood up again and the mother stood up with him, in cohesion. The man was saying something. He had long hair like a woman, the mother noticed now, as had the father once. *How had she not noticed this at first?* When the man pulled the cord the mower roared. He pointed at it, two long nails.

The mower's clamor seemed to nudge the sun. The air around them rippled.

The man began to mow the lawn.

A VERY LONG HALLWAY

The son had the TV up as loud as it would go. He'd hoisted the glowbox off the stand into his lap. He'd wedged himself between the wall and sofa. From most major angles a person passing would not see him in the room. When the screen went black between certain scenes or before commercials, the son could see his head reflected with a warp.

The son had spent all morning brushing his teeth and gums and tongue and still couldn't get this certain taste out of his mouth. There were matted knots in the son's hair the size of horse apples, though usually the son's hair was beautiful and straight.

The TV had a name but no one ever called it by it.

The son kept pressing the volume up button though he already knew it was as loud as it could be. He'd tuned into a certain movie on a certain channel that for some reason came in clear. On the screen, there was a woman, pictured only from the back. She wore a dress, tight and red like the fabric on the sofa. The dress was slightly translucent in a way that caused the son to feel aroused. The son did not understand arousal. The woman was walking down a hall. Her strange shoes clacked on the tile so loud around the woman and the son that he could feel it in his chest. The hall's walls were long and dark and smooth. The woman did not pass any windows, any people, hangings, doors. The skin of the woman's legs was bruised.

The son stayed in the TV room for three days, days counted unnamed. He felt air or fabric move around him, but he did not get up to see who or what was there. The son could not get up. All that happened was he watched the woman walk down halls. The TV movie did not break for commercials. The son had to think to even breathe. The son knew he wanted a roast beef sandwich but could not bring himself to get up and go make it—his stomach speaking words—writing words along his flesh inside him—ageless, lightless. The son could feel the TV's weight and heat burning deep and deeper through, warping layers, peeling skin. No one came looking for the son.

Over several hours the son managed to slip his fist around the TV's extension cord. With concerted effort and metronomic breathing over several further hours, he used his will to tug the cord out of the wall, the tendon of his arm meat seething with the heat of the cord curled up around him and the electric flood sent there inside it through miles of wires through the outlet to the screen, which when pulled as prongs out of the two holes made no stutter—the woman went on walking in the long light. In the light along the woman's dress the son could read small embroidered script of words he'd said or would say later, stitching down her, near her skin. The woman was getting older. Her hair molted from blond to gray

to black. It grew in inches parallel to her encased backbone, *thousands of elevators, strands in packs*. There was a wet spot between her shoulders, leaking.

At some point, in some hallway, the woman passed a door. She didn't pause or stutter in her walking. She didn't stop to try this passage in this unending hall after all these hours. Just as quick, the door was gone. The son had seen the door. The door was white with a white knob and had a number. The son could not think which one, though he could see it. The woman's new long bone-white hair dragged behind her on the hall tile.

THE SON'S FINGERNAIL

Looking closely at the son's nail—the ring finger on his right hand usually, though sometimes the left, and sometimes on a toe or chewed to slivers in his stomach—one could distinguish a certain shape that in certain kinds of light became another hallway or a wall.

Other times one could see the son himself there embedded with his face cracked down the middle on the run of weird cell-matter the son's disease had cut into the nail—*the gloss of certain weeks the son had spent upside-down or in a prism—the rings the son would one day wear—the blip—the years uncoming, the windows sloshed with sun.*

Other times there was absolutely nothing and you'd be a fool to think in wonder.

Look again.

POWER EXIT

The father lay on the bed. He lay beside the sleeping mother. Into his mouth he'd stuffed ten cigarettes. He gripped their gather like a bat. He inhaled through his mouth and out his nostrils. Filled with smoke, he fainted briefly—*a second smoke inside him*—and woke up. The house's power had gone out. There was no light from in or outside. The moon had moved behind something or another, or someone had blocked it, or it was no longer even there. The father's pupils began expanding.

In the bed the wife sat up. She asked what happened to the light. The father asked what did she care, she was sleeping. The mother said the light had gone off inside her sleeping also. She said she'd been talking to someone in there and they were looking at one another and happy and things were good and then the light went off and she could not find this person no matter how loud she called into the dark. The father said, How nice.

Through the air vent to the downstairs they could hear the son's voice, shouting, though neither said anything about it. The father inhaled his cigarettes and blew more into the cloud over the bed. The father didn't say anything further about the mother's sleeping or the light or what else they should do. The mother breathed the smoke without complaining. She didn't ask when he'd started smoking. She moved to get up out of the bed and the light in the house came on and she was naked.

The father had not seen the mother's body in a decade. He found her appealing still, despite her marks. The mother had been through long cycles of weight loss and gain. Some months the mother would eat as if there were someone else inside her. Some months she couldn't hold a glass of water. The mother's breasts were huge and white. The father felt his body stirring. The father raised his pelvis off the bed.

The son wasn't yelling anymore. The mother said something about the room seeming much smaller. The mother got back in the bed and covered up. She turned her back toward the father. Her back was ridged and knobby and had pockmarks all around it which when connected made a number. The father did not try to touch—he knew better—but still he kept his body flexed. He kept himself suspended as much as possible off the mattress and soon his muscles stretched with ache. It was a game. The sweat sluiced off his back onto the bed sheets. He was grunting. The smoke encombed his head. He could breathe still without coughing.

The lights went off again. The mother sat up. The lights went on and off and on in quick succession. Outside, they heard the sound of metal against metal. The mother went to the window to look down. She stayed at the window for some time, her breath all foggy. She didn't say anything about what was there. The father noticed now she had a scratch mark down the center of her chest.

In the hallway, the father heard the son talking in a strong, high voice. Then the son was laughing. He had a very peculiar laugh. The mother turned away from the window and went to stand facing the wall.

On the other side of the wall, though the mother could not see him, the son came into the adjacent room and stood. The mother and the son became parallel to one another, a wall between them. The mother moved her legs a certain way. The son moved his legs in mirror, spreading. There they held an endless posing pause—a wet erupting from the son's mouth, then the mother's, twin rivers glinting of a light.

Behind, the father watched the ashes fall off on his tired stretch-marked belly. He lit another pack. The lights went off and on and off and on. Their power bill would be enormous.

RELAX

Over many weeks, once they had settled, *their copies nowhere*, the house fell into feeling, often, fine. The house had an oven, stairs, some ceilings. The family began to loosen. They put their things were they belonged in this new system. They unwrapped the crap they used the most first, then on to baubles. They changed the grade of light in certain rooms. They hung up pictures of things they wanted to remember or identified with or just liked to look at while passing in the hall. The family tried to make the house their home.

As weeks gathered, passed in packets—days that often seemed of no uniform length, one unto the other and again—the house took shape around its new contents in name-less ways. Some nights the family would be woken by long bowed tones from all around—their whole house surrounded by *an edgeless, shapeless singing*; a *sound that had an eye*. It never seemed as though the family all heard the sound on the same eve-nings. Sometimes it would stir only the mother or the son. Sometimes the tone seemed,

to the father, just inside his eyelid—*therein, he could not stand up from the bed, his flesh repelled upon the air as if by magnets*. Some nights, the whole night, the tone would row, the mother and father there frozen side by side in bed together, seeing one another, not a blink. In the mornings, one or the other might mention how they'd heard it— the loudest droning—*the father thought it was a D flat, though he could not sing it back in tune*—and the one who'd heard it the night before would say, Oh, I slept straight through the hours.

Down the street three feet, or just above it, the sound around the house could not be heard.

Some nights, the son, awake well beyond both parents, would shake inside his skin. The sound would form around him, like cold clothing, threading on the night. The gong and organ in his chest would chime right in—repeating, harmonizing. The son felt words along his tongue. In the mornings, trying to tell the father or the mother of the shape growing inside him, all around the house, the words came out as something else.

Panes kept falling out of all the windows. Sometimes the sand that'd made the glass became apparent, insects sprawling in the grain. The tires on the family car would have flattened many mornings. The welcome mat would melt in too much light. The birdbath teemed and toppled. The dishwasher would seem to speak. Nothing ever seemed to line up with one another. The son could not walk from one room to another without bumping his elbow, nicking his shoulder. He often heard people speaking in the vents, grunting or gunplay on the roof. The house would not stay still.

The father and the mother tried to go on, despite the headaches and morning pus. They fixed the windows and kissed the son. They kept their cool. They did not scream at one

another when the garage door came down on the car while they were backing out. They did not panic when the front yard flowerbed spat the bulbs out of the ground. They did their best just not to think. Relax a little. They found themselves repeating it: RELAX. RELAX. They slept with their eyes open, all at once.

TWO

Live audiences frighten me to death.

SHARON TATE

WHAT TOOK THE FATHER SO LONG AT WORK

The next day it took the father six hours to get home from work. He took the same way he took home every day but each day it seemed to take a little longer. The streets went on a little further each time he drove them. There were new things on old streets. There were new streets with no signs for street names. There were traffic lights spaced barely yards apart. Certain lights would sit for many minutes red with the father edging the car further and further into the empty intersection. There never seemed to be any other cars. Ahead, the horizon of no dimension—limbless and suspended, several states away.

For a while the father could not hear anything around him—not even breathing, not even wind—except the sound of something dragging under the car, but each time he pulled over there was nothing. The car stereo would not make sound.

At one point on one of the streets the opposite lane filled with running dogs. The dogs were

black and had shining eyes and they were drooling from the mouths. The drool splattered on the windshield and made the street slick and the father skidded a little in his own lane. The windshield wipers made an awful screeching, as if soon the glass would break.

The drive home took so long the father got hungry two different times and at each he stopped at the same fast food restaurant and ordered the same thing, though the two items tasted very different. An attendant in one of the two fast food drive-thru windows had her eyes shut the entire time she took his order. There was a picture of the drive-thru window on her shirt and the father swore he could see himself sitting in the car outside that cotton window though the woman never turned toward him well enough that he could see for sure.

Q&A RE: THE FATHER'S CAR & HOUSE, ETC.

Finally in his driveway the father stopped and parked the car. He took the key out and he touched the key. The father saw the house. The father paused again and put the key in and turned the car back on and edged it closer to the garage. He moved as close to the house as he could manage without touching. The closer he got the car to the house, the more it seemed to shake. The father put the car in neutral and got out and put his head against the hood.

Q: DID THE CAR SOUND FUNNY?

A: The father could not tell. He was not good with his hands or with machines. To some this made the father not a man.

Q: WAS THERE SOMEONE IN THE CAR STILL?

A: The father didn't think to look.

Q: WHO WAS WATCHING?

A: The house had several windows.

Q: WHAT SHOULD THE FATHER HAVE KEPT IN THE GLOVE BOX THAT HE DID NOT?

A: A gun, a length of wire, a set of rubber gloves, emergency money and some form of rations, *Fear of Music* by Talking Heads, fake flowers (*the kind that never die*), permanent marker (*the kind that never can be erased*), a photo of his wife from a time he'd like to remember (*uh-huh*), a photo of his mother.

Q: WHAT WAS IT ABOUT THE NEIGHBOR'S HOUSE ACROSS THE STREET THAT THE FATHER DID NOT SEE, DISTRACTED AS HE WAS BY HIS OWN CONDITION?

A: The father did not see the enormous object wrapped in black plastic that took up the majority of the yard.

Q: WITH THE GAS REMAINING IN THE CAR, AND ALL OTHER GAS PERHAPS FOR SALE OR UNDERGROUND ELSEWHERE NOTWITHSTANDING, HOW FAR AWAY COULD THE FATHER GET FROM THE HOUSE IF HE DROVE THE CAR AT EXACTLY THE SPEED LIMIT IN ONE DIRECTION AND DID NOT PAUSE?

A: The father could not get far away at all.

WHAT THE FATHER DID THEN

With the car still on the driveway burning fumes, the father came into the house. He'd thought of something he needed to tell the mother. He'd thought of this thing earlier while staring into the work computer and had meant to write it down but didn't and now he was thankful it had reappeared, veined in his mind. It was an important thing. It was about the house.

The father could not quite say the thing aloud. The father slunk, eyeing for the mother.

The mother was not in the entry foyer, where in the early years she'd always met him coming in, her face engraved with home expression. As well, there, the father was used to seeing the family's shoes all taken off and stacked in order, as the mother was always a stickler for unsmushed carpet, but in recent weeks she'd stopped bothering to take hers off and so the son had too. The mother and the son both owned several pairs. The carpet was minced and feathered, brained already here and there with darker clot—some slush, some

blood, some body oils, a few bits meant to have been eaten. There were so many kinds of stains it looked like more than just the four of them in there, living. Three. Three of them, not four, the father corrected in his head.

The mother was not in the kitchen raising dinner. The lights were on and the fridge was open, full of light and frigid breathing. The oven had been preheated, though there was nothing in it and nothing sitting wanting to get in. A set of knives was spread out on the table. One of the four long bulbs in the overhead fluorescent lamp was dead.

The mother was not in the hallway that connected the kitchen to the garage, though from the garage the father could see his car up near the glass, its headlamps stunted by the near door and treating the tiny windows with more light. The father moved into the garage cracking his fingers and opened the freezer door and shut it. No mother, but the father found a hammer on the ice. The hammer's head was cold and solid, a thing that would always be. He touched the hammer to his face.

The father carried the hammer with him back into the family hallway with a set of school-made photos of the son ordered in ascending age on either side, a progression that ended with the most recent photos, which somehow still did not look the same as the son did now.

At a certain spot in the hallway on the carpet the father set the hammer down.

The mother was not in the laundry room where the floor had babbled sick with suds. Underneath the suds, the machine shook. The bubbles blew larger than most soap bubbles. The father stamped the sudding with his boot and heard it crackle like glass pellets.

The mother was not in the TV room, as far as the father could rightly see. There was a smell that curled the air. Some color not a color. The TV lay turned over on its face. The father called the mother's name several times into several cracks the room had and left his voice wedged there behind him.

The door to the son's room was closed and locked and inside he could not hear the son up or moving. Asleep, the father assumed, as the son would not answer, not for anything. He tried the knob again, again.

The mother was not in their bedroom. The bed was made and covered all with crumbling crap that'd come down off the ceiling, plaster popcorn. Something had been making the ceiling shudder in the evenings. The father's feet felt triple-sized. The father sat down to take his shoes off, glowing. The father said the mother's name some more. He was so tired. He knew that he should find her. He knew he couldn't just go to sleep, though he felt the feeling flooding through him, weighing his limbs down, thickening his blood.

The father leaned back on his elbows on the mattress, nodding. His head felt wide as nowhere. His head had so much in it.

The father heard someone rummage in the bathroom.

Ah, there she is, the father said, relaxing.

OTHER FATHERS

Outside the house inside the night beyond the father, the mother stood in porch light, in a gown. The mother knocked and rang the neighbors' bells. She banged and clapped and tried the windows. *People*, she thought. *People who can sleep*. The mother moved from one house to another. None of the houses looked like hers, nor the house she had grown up in, nor the house grown up in by the son. From house to house to house to house to house the mother knocked and crossed off numbers on her arm. She'd woken up and found the numbers there delivered, formed in the patterns of the clogged pores where her hair would no longer grow.

The mother had some idea of what she'd say when asked, if ever. Some homes had bells that shook her sternum, or would play a song she knew she knew. Some homes seemed to quiver right along, as would their home, leaning. The mother imagined herself inside each home's walls as she touched them—inside not sleeping, hearing herself at the door. At

certain doors she tried the keys she'd crammed fat in her pockets, but in the locks they'd spin and spin.

She guessed men's names into the crack, a string of fathers' names hidden inside her, *names of those who too had lost*. She tried Antoine, Paul, Stanley, James; she tried Tom, Kim, Ken, John, Jim, Ray, Edward, Robert; *she tried a name she could not quite name*. The names stuck to her mouth. These names came from somewhere in her, she could hear them, coming on and on, and trailing off . . .

The mother tried her name, then her mother's, then the father's, then the son's. No one would come. The homes went on hearing. The homes would stand there. Overhead the sky cracked up with old light—light that sometimes seemed to form a map. The neighborhood went on regardless, even when the mother hid her eyes.

THE SON'S PHONE

The son lay with his cell phone between his pillow and his head, the way the mother had made him swear he would. She'd bought the phone in case of relapse—*but relapse into what? The son could not remember.* He had to wear the phone on him at all times. *What if he could not find her?* The mother could not stop thinking. Sometimes in her thoughts the mother would explode as balls of heat and crud and light.

The son's phone was purple by most opinions, though sometimes it might appear blood red or translucent.

The son had set up a mirror at the foot of the bed that he could look in and see himself, as well as what might be in the room around him. So much of most rooms were never

watched. Many people had used this room before the son, the son knew. Sometimes he felt they were still there. Some mornings he would wake up and the mirror would have turned slightly, rotated to one side, which the son attributed to his sleep-kicking, learned from his mother, held inside her. Some mornings the mirror would be turned around entirely, so that the son woke to the mirror's flat brown back. Sometimes he'd find the mirror in other rooms inside the house.

There were sometimes other copies of the mirror.

The son also tended to talk in his sleep quite a bit, though neither he nor any other had heard anything he'd said while sleeping, ever. The sleeping son knew when to shut up. Most nights the son could not sleep at all.

The son concentrated on one body part and then another, approaching nowhere. The phone rang against the son's face. The son rummaged, found the ringing, and took it open. Inside the phone there someone spoke—someone not the mother. The son said something back. His voice felt chalky, caught inside him. Inside the house the house stood still. The someone took what the son had said and said it back just slightly different, sounding almost like the son himself.

The room was dripping. A string of stinking lights. The phone against his head, a squeeze of wires, warm as fire among day.

The someone went on saying the same thing over and over, warbled and rushing, in a loop. Within the loop, by slips in repetition, the voice took the tone of something else: a buzzing, beeping. It raised abrasions on the son's chest, the patchy pale skin puffing up with shapes like words. In the room downstairs, just below the son, the pucker in the

wall grew slightly bigger. In the mirror the son saw nothing. The silver surface had a little curdle.

The son could not get the phone off of his face.

The windows sweating. The skin along the son's wrists and forearms firming, fitted as with gloves. His cells, in sound, becoming ordered, torn up—the house inside the son so calm.

The son's arms felt deboned—fuzzy, how they'd felt in those sick months—months during which each night the man had appeared above his bed. The son had not mentioned the man to anyone, not his mother, even during all those weeks she'd never left him, never let go of his hand—not even when the man appeared right there beside her. The man had been there on the first day the son started feeling sick. He'd walked right up to the son in the cafeteria. A hairy man, with covered head. He'd come to the table and stood above the son and reached and touched the son across his face—his lips—his jaw. The man had slid his thumb into the son's mouth, just like that. He'd spoken through the finger, in a voice. The man with the yellow shirt neck pulled so loose. The man who'd stood and stood and stood, looking at the son until the son closed his eyes and he felt the fat crooked thumb expanding and when he'd looked again he wasn't there—just the whole long school room full of children eating lunches, silent—the adults against the school walls watching with their heads cocked—no one said anything about it, even after the man was gone. The next day the son could not sit up.

The son was certain this person on the phone now was not the same man as that man then, but he knew they knew each other. He didn't know why he knew that. He sensed something at the window but he refused to look. The man inside the cell phone had been talking all this time.

WHAT THE MOWER FOUND

The mother mowed the yard again. She mowed the yard, the yard, a prayer. The mother was slick with sweat and slather. Her skin was red in certain places from sun and where she'd scratched herself to keep the ants and bees off. The insects swarmed her head no matter how fast she moved. They had wings and teeth and eyes. They swarmed the yard, the street, the long horizon. The mother had mowed the yard twenty-seven times in the last week. Sometimes she'd go on for hours. Her biceps and pectorals were getting meaty. The grass was going dead around the edges from where the mother had pushed the mower so much. The mother kept her eyes wide and turned her head back and forth from side to side. Where was the man who'd fixed the mower? What else could he put a hand to? All those surrounding lawns on all those houses.

The father was still gone. That morning he'd left sometime just after 4 a.m. and he would probably not be home till after midnight. His face seemed to be sinking into his features.

The mother tried to think of the father's name. She could think of lots of other names it might have sounded like, but not quite the right one, she knew. She mouthed out things she'd said before—she reversed her rehearsed vows, teasing her tongue toward the father. She mowed the yard in wicked zigzags, reckless with her aim. The mower devoured her newer flowers—begonias, ivy, mums. They were dying anyway. She ripped up one long sod piece, spurting mud on the walk. Underneath the sod, the insects hung, spaghetti. The mother kept pushing, head up, chest out, scrunching her face best into something someone watching could sometime want.

The mother did not see the son watching through the window on the second floor where there may not have been a window once before.

The mower soon grew heavy. The handle hurt her hands. The mother went on garbled grunting, as if trying to push something from her insides. Around a corner by the chain fence, she felt the mower suck something up. Metal clanged against the blades. There was a whirring, choke and smoke. It spat something out its side. The mower whirred a little longer and then got tired, then was gone. The mother squatted on her haunches in the trampled mud-mushed grass, her eyes stung with gasoline and sweat, the sky behind her slightly hulking. In the grass there, slushed with clippings, scarred, the mother saw the egg.

THE COPY EGG

The egg was made of a smooth dark polymer with several seams and edges, though the mother could not make them open, try as she might with nail or hammer. Several hours of such tinker caused a burning at her eyes.

The mother found with effort how the egg did other things.

The first night she slept with the egg under her pillow, hugging. She woke with the huge toy in her mouth. Her chest felt funny and she could not remember sleeping. She later found the garage filled with an inch of liquid. The liquid stunk and had to be scraped out. The mother watched the father on his knees for hours scowling with the trowel.

The second night the mother hid the egg inside a lamp. She wasn't sure whom the hiding was meant to be from. She'd bought the lamp from a garage sale run by the neighbors. The stuff was left out on the front lawn with a sign. No one was watching. The mother left a dollar. She went back and left a dime. Later, she couldn't get the lamp to work. She liked the lamp—the look and stink of it, the pattern. She called it Bill. She sat it at her bedside. The egg seemed to fit the nodule where the bulb went just exactly. In the morning the lamp was on. The mother carried the lamp and egg into the bathroom and used the light to read while in a bath. The light made her feel younger, but not enough.

The third night the mother felt very tired and did not have time to touch the egg at all—instead she dreamt she ate it. She dreamt it had a job that paid for all. She dreamt it became a full-grown boy who sat beside the son and kept him clean.

The fourth night the mother stayed up late alone and held the egg against her chest. She found by lengths and rubbing how the egg could steer the house. When she touched the egg in one location, the downstairs bathroom toilet flushed. When she knocked with her left thumb knuckle on its one small gray abrasion, the egg nudged the kitchen off an inch. Other sorts of routine made the egg do other kinds of things, most of which would go unnoticed unless one knew exactly where to look. The mother found it difficult to remember which trick did what. She tried to write down notations, but her hand shook scribble. One thing the mother knew for certain was when she kissed the egg a tone would sound inside the shell. The tone triggered something in her brain that made her shake with vast orgasm. *It erased all previous tones.* Her body shuddered reeling, clobbered taut. The mother felt guilty and enormous. Her certain veins clenched into bouquets. It had been more than several years. The mother could hardly keep herself from squealing through the small house in the night—she had to bite a wooden spoon. She bit through it. She kissed the egg until

her eyes went bloodshot and her brain swam fat with glee. The next day she could not stand up. Nor the next day nor the next. Her lower muscles scored and knotted. The mother hid the egg inside her nightgown. She moaned with ache late into evening. The father went to sleep downstairs.

The mother cursed the egg. She called it Bastard. Inside the egg the egg changed colors. The next time the mother found the chance to kiss the egg it just sat and gleamed for hours. The mother spit. The mother put the egg inside a closet, covered, and closed and locked the door.

The fifth night the egg woke the mother up. Its voice rattled the bed frame and the mirror. A man's voice, deep and meaty. The father slept right on. The egg said things about the son—what he'd done and what would happen. The egg would not shut up. The mother found herself arguing with the egg aloud. The mother took the egg downstairs. She immersed the egg in high ice water. The voice bubbled upward, even louder. She got house paint and coated the egg's face in a new white—the same color as her bedroom. The egg started hissing. It melted through its outer layer with new blackened creamy flesh. It went on and on not only about the son now, but about the mother—who she'd been, what she'd wanted, how she felt about the father, what she would do given the chance with certain other men or even just for money. The mother's nostrils made little outlets, waiting for a plug.

The mother carried the egg out through the front door down the street past other houses. She searched for a sewer, but could not find one, no other holes into the earth. The mother ran, her sternum shaking. She became afraid others could hear what the egg said. She went back and got in the car and sat the egg on the seat beside her. The egg's voice super-boomed now, shaking the fake upholstery and the dash.

The mother drove the egg out to the coast. It was a sixteen-hour drive. The mother had never seen an ocean. The waves were flat and spackled, thick with old foam and floating geese. The mother lugged the egg into her arms. It seemed to weigh several times what it had, still growing. Halfway down and squeaming the mother had to stop and roll the egg in sand, its voice susurrating all the way out to the ruined dock.

At the smeared lip of the water—gassed and pudgy, melon yellow—the mother heaved the egg as hard as she could manage. It landed three feet from her feet. It fell in through the seahead spurting, as if in grease. Beneath the lip, it seemed to spin a minute, steaming. The mother watched the egg go down. There was a stutter on the surface. Overhead a troop of gulls quickly gathered fast—hundreds of them, enough to clot the sky. They dove in shifts at the egg's indention. Their beaks were long and weird and curvy. Their eyes spun in hungry loops. As they came up, they lunged for the mother, squawking. The mother did not flinch. The mother watched for quite some time to make sure nothing could be done. In the house somewhere far behind her were the father and the son.

WHAT THE SON DID WITH HIS INFORMATION

The son was in the kitchen when the mother came back in. The mother had grass clippings all clung to her body, stuck in the glisten of her sweat. She left a trail behind her on the carpet. She had it in her teeth too, where she'd licked the clippings, where several gulls had nipped her neck. She looked slightly like another person. She weighed nine pounds lighter than that morning.

The son had emptied the refrigerator. On the kitchen floor he'd spread the milk, juice, eggs, several cheeses, tortillas, bacon, cold cuts, margarine and butter, ketchup, lettuce— all the other things the mother had just bought. Everything had already either wilted or gone sour. Some had grown a slight rind of mold. The son had also cleared the freezer. He'd dumped the popsicles, waffles, yogurt, ice cream, ice in massive slushing piles. The

veal cordon bleu and veggie medleys and tiny cheesecakes in countless stay-fresh packets, an off-brand box of frozen dinners bought in bulk some evening for the son at his request. The melting had made a puddle that spread across most of the kitchen floor and turned the edge of the carpet leading into the dining room several shades of color deep.

The son had taken out the plastic and glass shelving and the drawers that held the food. The fridge was now one large empty box with two tiny light bulbs gummed with glow. The son was standing in the freezer part of the refrigerator. His shoulders fit the width precisely. The back wall seemed to stretch so deep. Just as the mother came into the room, the son moved his hand and closed the door. Their eyes met briefly in transition, like electric light. A shutter shut. The room was still.

Later the mother would wonder what would have happened if she hadn't come in at that exact moment. She would consider it a sign from god. She would seal the fridge with tape and bring another smaller fridge to sit in the parents' bedroom so that the son would not feel the urge to repeat. She would not think about how the son could just go climb into the freezer in the garage, or in the magic trunk stored in the attic, or how everywhere there were roads and overpasses, and cars driving under, piloted by whomever.

The mother went to the freezer and pulled it open and saw the son. The son looked tired, the same way everyone else she'd seen looked tired. Everyone everywhere at every moment as tired as they could be. The mother asked the son what he was doing. Her voice came out much higher than it did most days. The son said something wadded. The son had something in his mouth. The mother asked him to repeat. It came out more off. The son was trying to talk in the same voice as the voice that had called him on his cell phone, but the mother couldn't know that. The son had abrasions grown in beneath his hair that the mother would never find.

The mother did see, though, how the son now had long brown streaks worked under his eyes—so brown they looked like makeup. She rubbed one with her thumb and made a smudge. The son looked like a tiny warrior, or a linebacker. The son's eyes were whirling, as had the gulls.

Hey, the son said, staring at her. Hey. Hey. Hey. Hey. Hey. Hey. Hey. Hey. Hey.

The mother clasped her grass-green hands.

THE MOST FREQUENTLY PLAYED SONG ON THE SON'S COMPUTER BEFORE THE SON ERASED THE CONTENTS OF THE HARD DRIVE AND BURNED IT AND BURIED THE COMPUTER IN THE WOODS

1. _____ (197136 plays). This song's title appeared in the son's iTunes browser as a trail of mangled digits or a blur. The son could not view the details of the track. When the son tried to click the track to play it, iTunes would crash and often so would the computer. He did not know how the song had gotten onto his machine. Sometimes the son was able to mouseover the title when rolling in from certain angles and the album art would appear in the bottom corner of the iTunes browser. The album's artwork appeared to be the face of a man obscured by several kinds of light, though the son could never see the image long enough to be certain of the features, or the flesh. The song's play count rose week after

week, despite the son never hearing, and continued when the son turned the computer asleep or off. In this way this song covered the son's whole life, up to a point. Sometimes unplugged, the computer's encasement would discolor or spin or flake or walk. The son could not bring himself to delete this song.

INCOMING

The next time the father went to get the mail he found the whole box fat with caterpillars. They spilled out as he pulled the lid down. They were curled and brightly hued, some in a webbing. Some had hair as long as half a foot and fat as someone's finger. Some wore yellow and some wore orange, some wore gold or green and black or silver, messed in spindles, mounds. Some were a color the father could not think of the name of, though somehow it reminded him of a stretch of land for sale somewhere in Nebraska. The father had never been to Nebraska. The critters fell and wiggled on the concrete. There were hundreds of them stuffed inside the mailbox. There was no room for the mail.

The father went to the garage and got a cup and bucket and went back and used the cup to scoop the caterpillars out. He didn't want to touch them with his fingers—he didn't like that. Crawling. He didn't want to kill them either. The father had heard stories of men becoming things in other lives—how when you are reborn you could come as any other. You

could come back as a wall. The father imagined his father there in the mailbox now, spackled, wet with wriggling, and his father's father, and father's father's father, on from there. The father imagined all the prior men in his dead family there in the mailbox waiting for him, destined. This was some kind of delivery.

In careful scoops the father took the caterpillars from the mailbox and when he'd filled the bucket up he carried them away. He went off behind the house and through the forest following a wire until he got to some small exact place, in the mud. He dumped the bucket in a pile of colored moss or mold that'd grown up in this location, groggy bloom. The caterpillars (fathers) squirmed and squirted. Many slunk or screamed along the ground. Some submerged headfirst down into the dirt, building tunnels, which the father had never seen a caterpillar do, down and down into the earth. Then silence.

The father went back to the mailbox and filled the bucket up again. He hadn't thought there'd be enough caterpillars to fill the bucket twice. But the caterpillars filled the second bucket and a third and fourth and once again. He carried each load to the same place, the ground there darkening with every dump, rising up, *a structure*. By the time the father had carried twelve loads he was very tired and soaked with wetting and not so much interested in preserving the caterpillars anymore. He could hardly blink or breathe. He stopped and stood for some long second staring straight up into the long column of air carried above him, into the barely yellow sky, on pause—his spine inside him, hiding—his head's blood inside out and upside down.

If the father ever played a Hammond organ, he would find he was naturally a master. Elevator music. Careful evenings. Tone wheels in his heart and in his hands.

Moving again from the mailbox, the father went and uncoiled the garden hose from its

spindle set upon the house, its source mouth fed by pipes buried underneath the dirt. The father dragged the hose around the house. With the far end of the tangle he sprayed out the inside of the mailbox, flooding pressure, until it was clean and clear enough to kiss. On the ground below the mailbox the crap from all the gashing caterpillars pillowed and piled over. Their minor bodies gave off what looked like human blood, a little lake and many rivers. The warm ground seemed to sauté the runoff.

Several thousand gallons later—*in which a whole day passed, bringing the father full-scale back to the exact second of the day as the second in the day before when he'd stopped realizing where he was*—the father stood there for some time in waning sunlight and admired what he'd done. His hands had a slow itch. He craved chili. He scratched his hands together, knuckles in friction, and then he went inside and got online. On a credit card he'd never used before, *christening*, he ordered ten new magazines that would be delivered to his gorgeous, sparkling, brilliant, bending mailbox once a month.

The magazines were:

1. *Penthouse*
2. *Enormous Women*
3. *Better Homes & Gardens*
4. *The Father Life: The Men's Magazine for Dads*
5. [THIS MAGAZINE DOES NOT HAVE A NAME]
6. *2600: The Hacker Quarterly*
7. *Animal Husbandry Enthusiast*
8. *Teen People*
9. *TV Guide*
10. *Guide to* TV Guide

ENCOMBING

And yet the next morning, when the father came to the mailbox, he found it once again unclean. A new crop of caterpillars had convened around the post and swathed the unit with a fine tent of thready sheeting. The material was half-translucent so that through and around it the father could see the mass of caterpillars moving in arteries, some still gushing out the thread. The stunted light from overhead caused the bulb to sort of glow around the edges, melting the nest in places, dripping to the ground.

Near the center of the mass the texture became so thick that the father could no longer see the mailbox, nor could he really see the wooden stand that'd held its husk up, though he knew it had to still be in there, didn't it now, did it not? In this massive clot condition the mailman would not have anywhere to stick the mail, the father knew, not unless it could be wedged up in the larval sheeting, which made even the father's stomach lurch. The father would not receive any of his new magazines, he realized—he'd not be spending any of the

several coming evenings locked in one of the house's several bathrooms or large closets, studying the glossy pages of young famous men and women and whatever other things the magazines tried to sell—he would not receive that pleasure. He would get older every day.

In the street the father spun around all of a sudden, to recall how the air felt.

The father noticed then how coming up from the box the caterpillars had stretched their cocooning across the yard, a thousand tiny tightroped strings extended off the enmeshed mailbox to the dying tree that masked the front yard—which the father had asked be removed before the house was bought but then forgot—the whole gnarled trunk mostly exposed except for a couple bigger branches near the middle where the father had planned to hang a tire swing or something like it for his wife and child to enjoy, though he'd still not had time for that thing either, *his days stuffed thick with walking, needing, heat*. From the tree the caterpillars had begun to shoot across and comb over the house, their whorls of creamy thread just barely glinting in the waning slivered curtain of old light, as if covert, the thorax drizzle sloshed in long thin strands down through the branches across the long field of air onto the roof, encombing, jeweled with larvae—*further fathers*—spooling out around the house, reflecting light at certain angles hidden, a warbling quilt, a den.

WHAT WAS BENEATH THE FATHER

The father stood on the front lawn. Above the sun burped up and down. The father did not know he was not moving. Beneath the father there was grass. Beneath the grass there was root and rock and mud. In the mud were several sorts of other minor organisms, convened and still convening. In the mud there was cells from skin that'd been on humans and there was water that had come down through the air. There were things that'd died and fallen off of trees and floated down and decomposed and sunk into the soil to become part of the soil or to become the soil itself—*a single curving surface on which any flesh must walk or lay*. Further layers under, the dirt turned into rock, slathered in being, crushed with pressure, juiced in spots with gush or tunnel. Certain tunnels went very deep. Certain tunnels ended in doors that led to rooms.

13-DREAM DREAM SEQUENCE

That night the father slept through thirteen dreams. In the first dream he was a priest. In a second dream he was in Judas Priest. In a third dream he betrayed himself. In a fourth dream he ate so much spaghetti he exploded. In a fifth dream he was a beach towel in an unlit closet. In a sixth dream he was a woman who came to the closet and threw up all the spaghetti into the beach towel. In a seventh dream he was all the beaches and all the sand. In an eighth dream he had a cubicle beneath a certain beach where gorgeous women came and forced him to have sex. In a ninth dream he got folded in a rcmaindered library book and sold on eBay to a woman who binge-ate twice a week. In a tenth dream the father became a series of explosions in a video game his son was playing. In an eleventh dream the father felt very tired, though in this world *tired* meant *obese*, though *obese* meant *made of light*. In a twelfth dream the father was asleep and could not be woken no matter how long they screamed or what weapons were used. In a thirteenth dream the father woke and found himself above himself and inside his mouth he saw himself and inside that

self's mouth he saw himself and inside that self's mouth he saw a window, and through the window the father saw another window, and through the window the father saw mountains, fountains, fortunes, beaches, gazebos, grease, disease, and the father found that he was laughing and the father crawled inside himself and turned around.

SEQUEL

The son burned through the channels. The son saw ads for ground beef and cow milk and respirators. He saw men throw balls at one another. He could not find the woman in the hall. He'd forgotten even what she looked like—her shape—though she was always in his mind. In his bedroom in the mirror or in the air above his bed sometimes he felt he could feel her just beside him. He would move around his bedroom with his eyes closed, feeling for her with hands. She was there.

In absence of the hall film, the son became distracted with another. A movie made many years before the son was born. The son had seen this one before—when he was sick a certain channel had played it back-to-back for near a week—every time it seemed most new. The son couldn't tell what the film was about. There was a family living in a house. There was a father, a mother, and a son. The family all looked tired. Nothing ever really happened. The father drove places and got lost and walked around the house. The mother

mostly cleaned and worried. The son would stand and sit and stand. Other scenes showed the family together, going places, though these were rendered in black-and-white, and seemed of a different grade of film from all the others. Yes, this film was different than the other times the son had seen it.

This time there was something wrong inside the picture. The heads of the main actors and actresses were blurred, though they had not been so the other times the son watched the film, he thought. Also, in this version, the family all kept falling down. In scenes where they'd be walking, doing things the son remembered having seen them do in scenes before, suddenly their legs would fail and they would go down, or otherwise the house around them lurched. The characters did not make reference to this happening—they went on with the scene around the blips. Sometimes the camera fell as well. Sometimes there'd be whole rooms of people falling—all of their heads blurred—*actors*. A scene would take place in a mall, then suddenly all the people walking and shopping and eating fast food would just hit the ground, and then they'd get right back up and keep doing what they were doing. Sometimes the people could briefly be heard talking loud, but in a language that didn't make sense. The sky over the people would turn purple or turn reflective or begin raining ants or caterpillars out of large holes. No matter what happened no one in the movie acted any different. The son knew the film had not gone this way before. It had not lasted so many hours. The film went on and on.

The son had almost fallen asleep watching the movie before he recognized himself—saw himself right there in the movie, in a window in the background of the screen. His face, unlike the others, was not blurred. In the window the son looked frightened. The son's hair was flattened, of a bright white. The son could not tell what the window was a part of—the shot was too close up. Several other characters with the blurred faces blocked long sections

of the shot. The son felt he recognized certain bodies, the black holes of blurred mouths moving on pale heads.

In the window the son was saying something. The son couldn't hear him through the glass and other conversation, though he could tell by the son's lips that the son was repeating the same thing over and over. The son's lips were cracked and kind of swollen, the same lips the son used each day to eat and drink and speak and sometimes kiss another's skin. Then the camera moved and the son was no longer in the picture and the blurry heads inside the film went on—scenes and scenes there never-ending, and in some scenes other scenes there played in the background on little screens—and in the background of those scenes, screens too—and in those and those and those, so on.

Upstairs in the son's closet, the sealed black package rolled over on its side.

SPECIAL FRIEND

The son and the new girl quickly became special friends. They sat together in the lunchroom—no one else came near. That week the school stayed filled with screeching as the school tested the fire systems and the lights. The son could see other people talking but heard all siren. He could somewhat still hear the girl. The blinking shook his eyes. The girl paid for both their lunches. She carried both trays with one hand. The son was so hungry lately. After meals he chewed his fingernails and hair. The girl and the son had a lot in common. They both liked sleeping. They both liked knives. Some days in class the girl would stand up and put her gloved arms out and make a hum and spin around and the teachers never stopped her. Nobody ever said a word. The girl told the son there was something she had to tell him later. Sometimes the girl bought the son gifts. She gave the son a heavy book with empty pages. She gave the son a glass bead to sleep with. She gave the son lots of lengthy, pressured hugs. She said she didn't want the son to give her anything because she liked giving so much more.

BODY DOUBLE

Sometimes at school the son would come into a classroom and find himself already seated in his assigned chair, his hair combed clean and neatly parted, a blue word sometimes plainly scrawled or stamped across his creaseless, spit-shined head.

VERSION

Sitting upstairs in the closet, *where she'd hidden,* the mother heard a knocking through the floor—sound that seemed at first to come from on the wood there in the closet, just behind her head. *She could not move. She was so thick.* The mother, sitting wobbling, felt the knocking shift along the inseam of the house, all down around its back and belly to the downstairs, to the front door. There the knocking became pounding, became shouting, became bells—a chime the house had held inside it, somehow, since it had been built, a human sound. The low tone of the doorbell made the mother's body moisten, the stink of grass around her head—the knocking pounding all throughout her, at her heartbeat, twinned together, double time—then, inside the rhythm, she could see again, and she could stand.

At the door, through the thick peephole, the sweating mother saw a man. Not the man she'd hoped to see there, *he with such hands,* but her husband, balding. Here, the father, at his own door: a lock to which he had the key. The mother breathed to see the father upright,

glistening in outdoor light—she could not remember the last time she'd witnessed him outside the house since they moved in.

And yet this father was not the father, the mother saw then, looking longer, her brim shifting—no, not quite. This man clearly had aged less than the current father. His cheeks were tight and eyes were clean. He had another way about him. Kempt clothes, casual. A fine set of clean black driving gloves. The mother saw some kind of promise in his posture, days yet coming, the expectation of a life. For years all the males the mother looked at looked like the father—every single one—though that was in the years when he was thinner and she quicker and them strong.

The mother looked and looked and looked again, her eyelids flitting. This man was beautiful, she knew. Like her husband except newer, neater, which could have made him anybody.

The mother unlocked, unlatched, and opened up the door.

ACTIVE LISTING

Beside the man, the mother saw, as the strong door revealed another hole, there stood a woman, too. A woman about as tall as the mother, a small taut belly protruding from her skeleton, petite. This woman wore a veil—a white bride's veil, the mother noticed— certainly a bride's, it had to be, *the color shifting, pale*, with long dark driving gloves, like those the man beside her wore, covering her skin's arms. Through the veil the mother could see the semi-outline of the other impending mother's face, the features meshed in, fluttered. She had a mouth and, somewhere, eyes.

The mother smiled. A new young starting, she thought. One for another. She felt her skin inside her, warm.

The mother watched the other woman reach slowly on into her pocket, as for a gun. Together they inhaled, then.

The mother closed her eyes. She felt the warm air blowing somewhere high above her, though down here the air was still. She swallowed and she swallowed.

When she looked again, the other woman had a piece of paper in her hands. At first glance, it seemed blank, then it seemed to show the mother her own head back. The mother's dry eyes swam. She craned her neck in, stumbled closer, looking for her age. Up close, she could read there, a description of her house—the ad she'd placed just that same morning, black-and-white. How many bedrooms, their dimensions. How many fireplaces, baths. Kind of siding, year built (*left blank*), a/c presence, names of nearby schools and roads. The mother wasn't sure how the ad had already made print. The paper people had said it would take at least three days—days the mother had planned to use to clean the house, to mow and mow the grass. Most days the day was always over before the day began.

And yet here was this young couple, *local people*, at the front door, for a view. They looked clean and kind, dressed and possessed of a certain manner that to the mother suggested money, which suggested therefore that if they approved they might buy quickly, and then the family could move even sooner to a new house, which was beginning to seem more and more exactly what they needed. The mother did not feel at home. At night in their bedroom she had dreams of such condition she could hardly bring herself to go to sleep. Dreams of fissure, squashing, oily sneeze. Dreams of the son screaming and on fire. Of the sky above them melting like a raw egg and dripping down to crush the house with them inside it. During the dreaming the dreams seemed very real, not like a film at all, the way some dreams often would.

Though the father, in more recent days, had sagged in their decision to get out. Sometimes he seemed concerned with the same fervor as before—the sooner they were somewhere else, the better. He was not sleeping so well either, he complained, though through the

night, when home, he snored and snored and did not shake. The mother stuffed her ears with plastic and still could hear him blowing up with sound.

Other nights the father would shake his head and stomp for her even mentioning their moving, then wouldn't come to bed at all. From their room the mother could hear the father moving around inside the down and upstairs, banging and speaking, the sounds so faint at times they seemed more far away from her than the house was wide—the father barking in wordless fury on his way in or out the door. Some nights he'd bark so hard at such high volume he went hoarse and could not speak again for days. Other times no sound at all would come out, despite the fervor, all the wanting, in his eyes.

The mother's own eyes now in the yardlight stung, wet and glitchy.

The mother's body unlocked, unlatched, and opened up her mouth.

WELCOME

The mother welcomed the couple into the house. She did not ask where they'd heard about the listing. She ignored the sudden smell of dog. When they were all in, she closed the door quickly as she could behind them, though some of the bugs got in, as did air.

In the foyer the mother began to say certain things aloud. She walked the couple through the home, spreading her arms in massive gestures: *here*, *look*, *yes*, *oh*, *lovely*. The husband seemed to need to lead his wife around. The wife's body did not move much in any one direction unless directed. Her joints popped a little riddle *pop pop pop pop pop*.

The mother showed the young couple the kitchen where the mother had just finished putting away all the silverware, which for some reason had come out of the dishwasher more than a little stained—a deep bright brown that could not be washed or rubbed all off.

The mother showed the young couple the guest bedroom with the guest bed that for some reason looked newly tousled, though the mother had made and remade it just that morning, having found the father in it once again. The guest chest of drawers had been moved parallel to where it had been. The shower in the guest bathroom had been left running scalding hot, erupting steam.

The mother showed the couple the stairs to upstairs, the stairs with strip-striped carpet like no other location in the house, which never failed to make the mother dizzy no matter how hard she tried not to see.

She showed them where each night she and her husband tried to sleep.

God, the rooms seemed smaller with someone else there looking, looking.

The mother showed the couple the huge hall closet where the family kept their towels and sheets and a few old blankets and their winter clothes, which for some reason were always jumbled, and always fell out when the door opened no matter how carefully they were stacked, and for which, as it happened now, the mother cursed aloud and apologized as if that never happened, while the couple just stood there looking on. In her periphery, at some angles, the mother sensed she saw the couple wearing different clothes—long black cloaks or running outfits or pleated church suits, or none at all—though when she looked to see again there she would see they were wearing exactly what they had before. Sometimes the woman would be wearing a long locket around her thin neck, sometimes not.

Through the veil the mother could not see the woman's eyes. *Her eyes my eyes*—the mother thinking—which became replaced in the meat behind her nostrils with the shush of inhaled air.

The mother did not show the young couple the TV room where some certain smell had caked the carpet with a frosty fuzz, charcoal-colored, its surface pilling up in patterns, veins.

She also did not show them the son's room, though she knocked and knocked and tried the knob and called through the keyhole. Behind her, the veiled woman sniffed the air. She sniffed not as if from sniffles but from smelling something disagreed. The sniffing made the veil's fabric pucker against the woman's face.

The woman continued to stand beside the son's door even as the mother moved on to show another room. As the mother stopped and saw her hanging back, the husband stepped between. He pointed at the room with two long fingers, nodding. He smiled to show his teeth.

The mother knocked and knocked again and halfway shouted for the son. She felt her voice around her face, a little mush. The son had stuffed some kind of fabric into the crack beneath the door, letting no light through. The mother could not tell if this had been there when she first began to knock. Her forehead flushed with blood. She turned back toward the man, and looking past him, at the woman, explained the son was likely sleeping—said the son was a very heavy sleeper, which was true. The son had been sleeping more than ever lately—most days he went to bed and slept hard from the moment he got home until it was time to get up again for school the next day, unless the mother or the father woke him up and made her come do something nice like eat. The mother could not help going on and on, making excuses for the child, saying his name again and again in a slightly high voice, sweating through her shirt. She felt embarrassed. Her sweat had no odor at all, and traced the veins along her neck.

The couple lingered by the son's door even as the mother started to lead them away. The

woman stayed still, touching the doorknob. The man rubbed his eyes and took her by the hand. Throughout the house thereafter they kept on looking back in the direction of the son's room's location, even through the floors and walls and walls.

They did not seem to care at all to see the master bedroom, where they would sleep night by night by night by night by night, the mother mentioned, the word *night* falling out of her mouth in repetition, *she could not stop it*, and still they did not say a word or blink.

They did not look askance to find the master bathroom's mirror again off its putty, leaning forward above the basin making double image of the floor.

They did not seem to smell the smell of something musty coming from the vents there, the mold loosening all through the house, suddenly warm.

Their foreheads folded slightly at the child's bookshelf, packed fat end to end with colored spines, *though while awake and of his knowledge, the son had only ever read one book—a volume given to him by the father's father, unbeknownst to either parent, a strange, enormous edition with only one letter on every page, to be read along a slow strobe. The son had found he could quote the text at length before he'd read it. When he did read blood would leak out of his nose. It would pour onto the white pages, blanks, making new letters, then, on closing, smear them doubled, smudge the letters into more.*

The couple moved so slow all through the house, like lava.

A bell inside the house was ringing, though the mother could not hear.

This is where on the weekends my son likes to sit and tan her skin, the mother mentioned

in the kitchen, pointing through the door glass at the yard and swimming pool. *His skin*, she corrected, not *hers*. My son is a boy. She said how good it felt for children to go swimming. What clean work water could do.

The couple appeared blank. The mother shook her head, began again. Hello, yes, welcome, please come in now, I'd love to show you our fine house. The flushing mother started to open the door to lead them out to where the pool was, to have a closer look, but then thought of something and stopped and stopped again. She turned to press her back against the glass. Actually they couldn't see the swimming pool today, the mother explained, aching, as it had just been treated. It wasn't right to breathe. The couple did not press this issue. They continued not to blink or budge or motion or say much of anything at all.

HEY

Hey, what's your due date, the mother asked at some point, on a whim. She asked with a strange expression on her face. She didn't know she wore the expression and didn't mean the thing the expression seemed to mean she meant. They'd gone through the whole house already and were back in the first room where they started, with the couple standing close together, arms at their sides. The mother was standing near another window when she said it, the whole back of her head and spine aflush with light coming down into the house from outside, though in the outside now it was night, and there were no streetlamps and no moon or stars. There was nothing, not even the yard.

The couple's mouths were closed.

The mother made a motion at her own midsection as if there were a bigger belly there—

where the son had been upon her sometime and now was just the air. She nodded between the blank space and the woman, drawing lines out with the motion of her head.

The man looked hard at the mother, shook his head. He shook his head so hard it briefly blurred. Stopping again, he looked older.

The mother's mouth continued moving without sound. She touched her own face, which felt like anybody's. She felt her jaw pulse in its gristle.

The man touched the silent woman on the back.

She's sickly, the man said. His voice was so small, sticky. She's not been feeling well. It's been known to go around.

The woman sniffed and sniffed, like wanting food.

It's been known to go around, the man repeated.

The mother tried to smile, made little sounds. She sort of curtsied the way young girls used to when wearing dresses—the way she had on several occasions in the past though she could remember none of them specifically right now. The curtsy made her hips hurt. She cleared her throat and turned, as the man had, away, to face the window, fat with glare. She said something nice about the window's size and the view through it—**that bright light**—the way she'd seen all the listing agents on those home shows do on the TV, as what could sell a house but a window.

3 DOORS 1 ROOM

Upstairs again, by request, the mother showed the couple the bathroom that the son used every day. The door to the son's bedroom from the hallway still was locked. The corresponding bathroom was small and had two doors that came into it side by side on the same wall. One door led in from the hallway. One door led to the son.

The son's door was locked as well from this side and further knocking went unanswered—though now the mother was really knocking hard and kind of shouting into the gap, so much so that the couple began to look into her with the eyes behind their eyes, making a memory of the moment that would last a lifetime and forever—held inside their heads. The mother felt concerned. She did not know why the son would lock the door while sleeping. She tried to think the right thoughts to keep her calm until the couple left. Everything would be fine, be fine, fine be, she said, inside her, and a little bit out loud.

The son's bathroom had a third door leading into a section with a toilet and a sink. The mother hadn't meant especially to highlight this portion of the house, though as she stepped inside and turned around she found the couple had followed her into the tiny stall space, all of them crowded in together. Their three heads were nearly touching. There was no more room to move and make more room. The mother noticed how the man's breath stunk of charcoal. She couldn't help but cock her head. The man was looking at her, breathing. He had both hands pressed at both walls, holding himself up. The mother didn't want to say they should leave the room now because what if the man knew about the odor and thought the mother was being rude—then they might not want to buy the house. The mother made herself continue talking. The mother reached around the woman's gut—*nothing at all there inside it, she imagined*—and pulled out each of the little drawers set in the washstand, revealing tampons, q-tips, blush. One of the drawers had a bunch of hair stuffed in it and the mother closed it quick. The mother said something about market value. She said something accidentally in French. She felt her torso getting lighter. The three bodies' collective assemblage of six nostrils quivered in and out.

The man touched the mother on the arm. Certain of the man's fingers were very cold—as if they'd been in an ice chest somewhere, years—while others in the same grip were crispy, warm. The mother did not recoil from the strange touch. He looked into the mother's eyes. His pupils resembled little stickers, the kind placed on placards when art is sold.

The man spoke toward the mother's skull. He said his wife needed, now, please, to use the bathroom. The woman, behind her veil, looked straight ahead.

The mother tried to say something and then could not and felt embarrassed again, rushed, and so nodded and followed the man out of the smallest room inside her home into a slightly larger room inside her home. The mother and the man together turned around

and saw the woman still there in the son's bathroom, standing staring at them, arms tight at her side.

Outside the room the man stepped up and pushed the door closed. He turned back to the mother, smiled.

The mother heard the woman turn the lock.

BEEP PROBE

Outside the bathroom, partitioned cleanly, the man and the mother stood spaced feet apart. The mother thought to say something but could not think of what or how. The man stood with his hands clasped in front of him and turned to look at the wallpaper. He leaned his head near to the wall. The mother watched him watch. His gaze was rigid and unblinking, staring straight on into surface. He seemed to be reading something. The mother moved to look as well. The wallpaper was a deep purple with deep purple ridges and tiny buttons in relief. The ridges' texture was rather soothing. The mother felt her body limp a little. The skin around her eyes grew moist.

She was not crying, not exactly.

The man was radiating heat. He had the smell of grass about his breadth, strong arms like the man who'd fixed the mower—*and like that man, this man, too, was gorgeous, if with a*

rash upon his cheek. A sudden stink of slit grass and motor rubbings made the mother's body lump. She started to ask something, blushing, but her mouth was closed and time had passed.

Behind them, in the bathroom, the other woman made a sound. A shrill, quick beep, a mouth noise, as if emulating some alarm, or some detector. There was a kind of pitter-patter. Then breaking glass, and wood against wood. A light showed underneath the door's lip. The woman's ever-moaning, saying words. The beep continued, high and awful, re-repeated, each iteration slightly shifting, until, in the mother's ears, the noise became to have a frame—began to take a shape of language there around it. The beeping, at her head, became a name. The son's name. Son's name. Beeping. The woman making, again and again there, the title of her child. The word she'd placed on him from nowhere, that had occurred as lesion in her sleep. The woman screamed the name into the walls among the houselight, in the smallest of all rooms, curdling the air. Beeping. Beeping. Name. Name. Name. Name. The mother felt the blood inside her turning hard. And just as quick, the name becoming something other: becoming ways she could not recognize—the utter shifting off from where it'd held him and slipping therein off into a struggling string. Not a name but something troubled. Reaching. Burble. The scream so loud by now it shook the house.

The hair along the mother's arms was singing. She closed her eyes and swallowed in the sound. Then, just as quick again, there was no sounding. Silence—or something so loud or strung out there was nothing to be heard. The house as still as any.

The mother turned around. She moved toward the door where in the smallest room the woman was not moving—*so still it could not be.* She knocked politely on the door's face, then immediately again.

The woman did not answer. A bigger silence. Some nothing larger than the house. The mother opened up her mouth—and again there came the beeping, this time louder, jostling the door, her hair, the ground. The shaking made the mother dizzy, and yet she could not stop—she could not close her mouth.

OTHER MOTHERS

The mother turned toward the man—the man right there behind her, breathing.

She's sick, the man said again. His voice was clear among the noise. Sick, he said, distinctly. He did not seem concerned.

He splayed his hand on the wallpaper, singling fingers.

This is words, he said.

The beeping felt, under the man's voice, somehow very far away.

The man ran his thumb along some lines. He read aloud in a strange language, what the bumps said. His skin glistened on his head.

Under the speaking, by the beeping, the mother heard the broken glass inside the locked bathroom getting crunched, as if under some other bigger object, like the woman, *another wanting mother, one day to be*. More jostling around, cabinets slamming, spraying water. There was the sound of sawing or other friction on the wall between the tiny bathroom and the son's. The mother spoke into the door's face. She tried the handle with her hand. The door, for sure, would not open. A door in her own home.

The man behind her, rubbing the household, its wallpaper, read aloud another line. These words came through him as more beeping, forming chorus, though now the mother, inside her, could understand. She could hear the voice as if it were her speaking. She fought within her to form breath. Doors inside the house. Doors in other buildings. Windows, vents.

The mother turned inside the sound to shake the bathroom door's knob with all her fingers. She tried to think of the woman's name so she could call it out, then realized she did not know the name at all. This woman could have any name.

She could be Janice or Doris or Euphrasie or Kathleen. *The mother had this list of names inside her again, female: other mothers.* She could be Mary Anne, Sally, Barbara, Arlyn, Mary, Jan; she could be Grace, M., Linda, Regina, Anna, Annie Ruth, Phyllis, Polly, Addie, Afeni, Cherry, Salomea, Joan, Komalatammal, Doreen . . . the names came on and on, in spinning, as for combinations on a lock. The mother tried to say the same name as her name, or her mother's, or the father's or the son's, but she found she could not recall any of those names. Her breath sizzled inside her. She leaned into the door. She squeezed.

These walls aren't even here, the man said behind her.

The man took her by her hand.

The mother started to rip herself away but the man's hands' grip was strong and now the fingers were all warm—blistering, even. She felt wet all up in her buttocks and her navel.

The man stretched the mother's arm and placed her hand against the wallpaper. The ridges slightly writhed. The man's gone eyes.

Feel, he said.

She felt.

the house there all around her, laughing

all through the roof and walls, the sound

in light, the child's name rerepeating

names in names in names on names

VOW

The mother loved the couple. She wanted them to have the house.

She wanted them to move in and live there right now. There was room. They could share the space together while she and the father looked and found another house. Or, perhaps, the mother mentioned, with her eyes closed tight inside her head, all of them could live together in this air together. They could be two mothers and two fathers, or whatever. All of them in one.

That is ridiculous, to think that, the mother said aloud just after, and yet knew some small to large part of her meant what she had said, and did not wish she didn't. She could not remember the names of even just the people in her family, much less anybody else. All of these words together in the mother's head, and still the beeping. A furry evening, all this light.

The mother lay face down on the floor.

She lay face down with arms splayed out beside her and listened to the air inside the home's vents gushing, coming out to feed her, warm.

OFFER

When the father got home from work that morning, the mother was in the kitchen. She was sitting at the counter on a tall stool with her legs crossed and her back toward the door. He seemed to not have seen her in months, or years. The father knew the mother would not believe his explanation that the streets were getting longer. He'd been getting up earlier and earlier to make it to his desk on time and his desk kept getting smaller and he kept getting home later and later and his fingernails kept growing. The last several nights the father felt sure that he'd come home, gone upstairs, taken off his clothes, gone to the bathroom, splashed water on his face, gotten into bed on one side—*he had not noticed the presence or absence of his wife*—rolled over on his side, gotten out of the bed on the other side, gone to the bathroom, splashed his face again, put on the same clothes, walked out the door. It took several full tanks of gas to get to work and back. The father had clocked the distance on his odometer and it always stayed the same.

That night on the way home he'd stopped and eaten books at a restaurant he'd never seen. The restaurant was next to another building he felt sure he recognized, as it had an unusual shape. He knew the second he saw the restaurant that he would eat there. He'd given up on trying to make it home in time for family dinner. He was so mother-fucking goddamn hungry. The restaurant had no sign. The tacos were delicious, the best he'd ever had. He couldn't even think of how a person could make a taco that tasted like these—they seemed to contain the pleasure of a whole meal in every bite. In each bite of the taco the father tasted steak and onions, ranch dressing, chocolate cake, bananas, gummy spiders, rum, and Cheetos. Those things all together tasted somehow very good. He'd ordered extra to bring the mother some so she could try them but after a while in the car he'd gotten hungry and he'd eaten them and he felt awful and too full, but would have done it again given the opportunity—given even thirteen hundred complimentary tacos, he would have eaten every one. The father had a new favorite place to eat and he planned to keep it to himself.

The father was walking up behind the mother. He moved slow, trying to be quiet, though he knew she knew that he was there. He found himself walking on his tiptoes, slow and lurching, like a man who'd come to kill. The father put both hands across his mouth to keep from giggling. His teeth bit at his one hand and he was bleeding and the blood was in his mouth.

The mother at the counter hunched and cringed with the father's every step. She felt afraid—afraid not for the father's silent acting, though she could sense it, but because the couple had made an offer and she didn't know what he would think. The phone had begun ringing almost as soon as she'd closed the door behind them. Within the hour a contract had been delivered in a black envelope by a private courier who appeared to have approached the house on foot. They'd offered the full asking price, in paper money. After-

ward, the mother felt so cold. She put on as many layers as she could manage, the oldest clothes stuffed in her drawers—dresses, shirts, pants, shoes she hadn't worn in ages—back before she became pregnant with the child. With so many layers laid around her she could hardly move her arms or legs, her body, heat amassing in her thighs, so large, though inside her, at the center, her stomach roared.

Behind, the father moved closer and still closer. The father's mouth drooled, overflowing. He had his hands worked into weapons. He closed his eyes.

When the father reached the mother he put his head square in the center of the mother's back. He pressed with his forehead in a way that made the mother's muscles stiffen, through the fabrics. They hung there slightly humming, their two bodies perpendicularly aligned.

Without turning to look at him, without surprise, the mother lifted the offer paper off the counter. She read it softly to the husband like a bedtime story, her voice rather raspy and unconcerned, feeling the sulk and burn of coming crying making her whole throat run with slush. The father's body tensed against her as she spoke the couple's offer's words, the formal language. The mother felt the father remove his head and stand straight up. There was a grubby guzzling sound then, as if inside him the father were compacting trash.

The father reached across the mother's shoulder and took the contract from her hand.

In the smallish light there in the kitchen for a minute the father seemed to stare straight through the paper. If he had seen through the paper, the father might have seen a person at the window. The father's hands were shaking. He found himself already holding a pen, the logo of the place where he'd eaten dinner kissed upon it. The father moved to press the paper flat against the mother's back.

Through her flesh the mother felt the father sign a name—not quite his name, she could feel that—the loop of lines and dots and holes went on so long.

The father crossed the other name out and tried again. He signed another, this one in big block letters that more resembled hieroglyphics. The father barked. The father's hand was cramped and jiggling and he could not hold it still. With his free hand he gripped the wrist of the one he used for writing and in long forced crooked half-strokes he this time finally felt his hand scrawl out his given name, syllables for years he had been stalked by, concentrating, pressing hard, causing small hash marks on the mother's skin, and underneath, the vessels breaking, giving blood.

When he looked again, it still was not what he'd intended. He'd made a mess of rods and dots, some of it written not upon the paper, but the mother's clothing, and through the layers, on her skin. He looked and looked at what he'd written.

That really *is* my name, he said aloud. His voice was soapy, like a car wash.

He put the pen down and closed his eyes and moved and heaved the mother from the stool, into his arms.

COPY SPEECH

Clordbedded ahst forb, said the father, alone upstairs. He had his head against the bathroom wall. He could not remember how he'd gotten through the house back to the bathroom. Froth hung in long ropes from his mouth. Blossbit ein vord cloddut, he said, choking. Cheem cheem murd bot. Loif oissis oissis oind.

There was a music in here with him, all of woodwinds and deep bass. He could feel the pen inside him, writing.

Unk barnitt weedumsissis, quoth the father, eicheit undit pordrondoid blerrum misht. Misht eichlitt leichord nord ip beebit. Juinfurr hossis, mekkum dha.

He could not feel his hands.

On the other side of the wall, in the guest bedroom, someone had hung a picture of the father. A pleased pre-father father at a party in nice clothes, surrounded by bodies, open-mouthed. They were together singing or saying something.

Behriddit meemle boikend, the father said. He could remember that night inside the picture like it was this one, in his skin. Borkind. Borsis borsisisis. Messalond.

Through his voice, in replication, the father heard now someone pounding on the door. Pounding so hard the house around him wiggled. The father stood straight up and looked around. He'd stripped. His pubic hair was bright white. His thumbs were bleeding and on the floor around his feet he'd made a symbol out of toothpaste. The small twitch inside his eye again. *A party.*

The person at the door struck four times, four times, four times.

Fine. I'm fine. Logborsis, the father shouted. He wiped his thumb blood on his gut. Busy cleaning. Nothing's the matter. Go on a minute. Slarsords. Almost done.

The father turned toward himself therein reflected, in the mirror, through the wall. He saw himself seeing himself, and then himself seeing himself seeing himself, copied, copied, on. His eyes inside his forehead looked so small—surrounded. Inside, his skin went on for miles.

In the bathroom the father saw his many selves reach up to turn the lights off, and the father saw the dark.

BELL CHORDS

The doorbell rang again all through the morning and into gloaming. The mother ran in fits. Each time she went to the door expecting—*him, he, that one, which one, who?*—and each time found someone other, someone new. Folks arrived in line with checkbooks, holding hands. Sometimes there'd be several families waiting. Each, as the mother brought the door opened, walked in proud, already home. Though the mother felt strongly about the couple's offer, she gave tours anyhow. She showed. She baked scones with black molasses and passed them on tiny plates, which the people took and smiled.

By the time most people left, their expressions had scrunched and darkened. They went from bubbly to still. Though nothing particularly bumming happened—no carpet sizzled, no paintings moved, the rooms' wallpaper did not peel—as soon as any buyer had been through one or two rooms apiece their eyes began to swim with blank foreboding. Their

cheeks sunk, glazed and pocky. Good natures became terse. Hands stayed in pockets. Dry lips. Some spoke of hearing cymbals or a pressure in their chest.

And yet each person who came to see the home by the next day had made an offer—some as large as two or three times what the father and mother asked—enough to buy another house plus many other things. The house was wanted. There was wanting. People left long garlands at their door. They brought cake and wine and called for updates. Who what when where why when how would they know who what when what was going to have the house. The mother bit her lip and wrung her hands. She had their lawyer put forward motion with the couple now on hold. She liked the couple—*knew them*—but now, more money. She praised god they'd not yet signed. Into the evening, sensing their fortune, the giddy mother went around and polished doorknobs and floors and faucets until she could see things in the shine.

The family all slept straight through the next several days, contorted. They did not hear the ringing phone. At certain points their eyes might open, not quite seeing, while all around the house went on.

COPY SLEEP

In his sleep the father saw the copy father in the room beneath their room. The copy father stood with both hands clasped behind his head, as if hunching for explosion or a sit-up, though the remainder of his body remained taut. The copy father hung an inch above the ground. The copy father looked up through the floor between them with his eyes stuck on the mother in the bed. The mother had moved to sleep so that her feet were on the pillow and her head was somewhere tucked down tight beneath the covers. The father could hear her grousing, breathing sickly and all wet. She kept asking the same knock-knock joke question over and over again, never getting to the punch line.

The copy father wore a yellow mink coat and a choker necklace with diamonds larger than the father had ever seen. Had the father received his copy of the current issue of *Enormous Women*, had his mailbox not been swarmed with bugs, he would have seen this exact getup

on page forty-four. The father would have recognized the woman in the picture, though he would not be able to name her name.

The copy father spurted gobs of water from his mouth. When the water hit the copy father's chest it sizzled, and when it hit the kitchen floor it sunk right in.

In the backyard—through the kitchen window, through the floor—the father in his bed saw so much light—as if someone had dragged the universe into Adobe Photoshop and bucket-filled the sky a nonexistent color. Most other nights, even in the day, were nothing like this—burst beyond seeing, beyond size.

In the father's sleep the house was exactly as it was on most days except when you opened the door that led to the garage instead of a garage there was another house made of blue flowers that you could go inside or eat, but the father did not see this room—he just knew that it was there. In his sleep the father could not move. His arms were soldered to his sides. His shoulders were pinned back on the mattress and his feet felt very large.

Through the floor the father watched the copy father climb the stairs.

Through the walls the father could hear the copy father breathing in the hall. Heavy, labored breathing. It shook the bed frame and the lamp. It shook the mother in the bed beside him and she was laughing. She sounded high, shook with a shudder in her extra clothing and her fat. The way she breathed in with the copy breathing made him feel hazy, grazing, tired.

The copy father stood outside the master bedroom with his face against the door.

SOMNAMBULIST

In her sleep the mother heard someone at the bedroom door and she stood up out of the bed. The mother walked to the bedroom door and listened. The mother nodded, cracked the door. On the bed behind her the father's mouth and eyes were open, though he did not blink. The mother saw the father shudder.

The mother left the bedroom and walked down the hall and stairwell and outside. Overhead the night was full. Overhead the night had opened and all throughout it there were words. Words made of skin or spit or coffee. The mother followed one certain sentence through the sky in a straight line. The mother walked on mud and gravel, concrete, glass, and stone. The mother's feet began to bleed a trail.

The sentence led to the front door of a house. The mother went in through the front door and locked it shut behind her. In the house the lights were off. Black lights, floodlights, stacked in masses. Several billion unburned bulbs. The mother went into another room. She went into another room. In the fifth room there was a glow and someone standing in the corner.

Long white walls.

Sleeping bees.

The mother left the house through a certain window some time later, leaving blood marks on the sill.

The window led into the backyard. The backyard was full of sand. The mother walked into the sand up to her hipbones. The mother folded her flat hands. With the grace of nowhere, the mother tucked her chin against her chest and fell headfirst into the sand.

Inside the sand there was a door. Through the door there was a hallway. There again the mother slept.

INVOCATION—INVITATION

In his room awake now the son sat hunched over her computer typing into a chat box with a 45-year-old man. The 45-year-old man had contacted the son via a social networking website that the son did not know he'd joined. The son and the man had exchanged email addresses and written back and forth for several weeks. The last email from the 45-year-old man in the son's inbox bore the subject heading RE:RE:RE:RE:RE:RE:RE:RE:RE:RE:RE: RE:RE:RE:RE:RE:RE:RE:hi.

The 45-year-old man said he had a wife and an ex-wife and two kids about the same age as the son. He said he lived nearby.

The son was not aware he was online. The son felt like he was sleeping. He didn't realize any of the things he'd said to the man in all those emails.

The son had told the 45-year-old man things he'd never thought he'd tell another, things he
didn't even know were true until he typed them, until the words were coming from his hands.

He told the 45-year-old man about the knife he'd stolen from the small store in the mall,
and how from there he could not stop himself from stealing knives wherever he went; how
he'd taken more than two hundred knives from different places in the past several weeks
alone and he had them all there in his closet; knives from restaurants and shops and other
homes; straight razors and safety razors and kitchen knives and plastic knives and steak
knives and pocketknives and knives emblazoned with special logos and with his own name
and Ginsu knives and knives for scraping and knives for fighting and butter knives and
butterfly knives and a knife he'd taken out of a blind man's hand in the street.

The son had told the 45-year-old man about the night he'd taken his father's car in the
sudden idea that he must drive, a sudden image of some warm location appearing at sudden
to him with the hottest shower spraying hard against his head, a place that *right now she
must go*, and in the night he'd went and had been driving, though he could not see over the
dash, and how he'd felt his body moving fast across the land toward that lit spot calling for
him to come forward, to move into its hull and stay and sleep, until suddenly from in the
fold of darkness there appeared an enormous gleaming dog, a dachshund several times the
average size, and how it had come unto him so fast even in unseeing that there was no time
for him to spin the wheel, and he'd hit the dog and heard it go underneath the car and there
was squealing and blood had sprayed over the glass, the son had become so shook up she
couldn't stop the car or take his cold hands off the wheel and he kept driving without slow-
ing, he drove and drove, and when he found he'd somehow gotten home again he washed
the blood off of the car, he scrubbed the car's skin with baby diapers, the way he'd seen his
father do, taking care, and though the blood came off the car it would not come off him and
it did not smell like blood.

The son had told the 45-year-old man what he wanted one day in a wife though the son didn't know quite what he meant by what he said.

The 45-year-old man had been asking for the son's cell phone number but the son had not yet let him have it. Please, the man kept typing. Please. Please.

The man had sent the son strange pictures of a light.

The first name the man had given as his real name was as well the name of many other people.

Now the son was typing and typing to the man in the chat box. He was also looking through websites for pictures of buildings laid to ruin—buildings beat apart by wind and weather, or hit by lightning or burned with fire. He didn't know why he wanted to see those things, but by now he had a drive full. They were there inside his computer. They were in there, copied on and on.

There beside the chat box with the 45-year-old man, another chat box opened. The message said, HELLO. The son did not recognize the screen name, **HELLO444**. He minimized the message. It popped right back up again.

    HELLO444: I KNOW YR THERE.

    HELLO444: I KNOW YR READING.

    HELLO444: I CAN C YOU THRU YR SCREEN.

The son waited. He was looking. He stretched before the panel. A small icon in the corner said **HELLO444** was busy typing. The son watched the blinking cursor on his end. He stood up and went to the window and looked down on the street. There was some mud there, moonlight, other houses. He stared a moment, somewhat transfixed. He heard the message chime immensely, a thousand tiny phony bells.

The son came back to his computer and saw another message, and again.

> **HELLO444**: IN THE FAR BACK CORNER OF THE ROOM IN THE HOUSE WHERE YOU LIVED BEFORE WHERE YOU ARE NOW THERE IS A VERY SMALL LATCH SET IN THE FLOOR OF THE ROOM WHERE YOU WOULD SLEEP NIGHTS EVEN THOUGH THIS ROOM WAS NOT YOUR ROOM. IF YOU LIFT THE LATCH AND PULL THE LID BACK THERE IS A LITTLE PASSAGE JUST BARELY BIG ENOUGH FOR SOMEONE YOUR SIZE TO SQUEEZE THROUGH AND IF YOU CLIMB DOWN FAR ENOUGH AND THINK THE RIGHT THING YOU WILL COME OUT IN ANOTHER ROOM.

> **HELLO444**: IN THIS ROOM YOU AS A PERSON SPENT MANY HUNDREDS OF HUMAN YEARS. YOU GREW INTO SEVERAL DIFFERENT VER-SIONS OF A MAN, SOME ENCHANTED, SOME QUITE BORED. AS YOU LEARNED TO LEAVE THE ROOM THROUGH MANY WAYS OTHER THAN HOW YOU CAME, YOU FOUND PASSAGES TO OTHER ROOMS CONTAINING OTHER PEOPLE AND YOU HAD MANY WIVES AND YOU WERE VERY WEALTHY. YOU LIVED IN SPLENDOR FOR LONG EONS AND YOU WERE WISE AND YOU WERE WANTED. THERE WAS NO CEILING ON EARTH THAT

COULD CONTAIN YOUR HEAD AND WHEN YOU TOUCHED YOUR
HEAD WHOLE PLANETS DIED.

HELLO444: WHEN YOU GREW OLD ENOUGH YOU WERE GIVEN THE GIFT
OF A SMALL OCEAN IN WHICH YOU BATHED FOR FURTHER
HUNDREDS OF HUMAN YEARS AND YOU GRANTED WISHES TO
PEOPLE WHO CAME TO SEE YOU THOUGH SOME DID KNOW
THAT YOU WERE THERE, AND YOU APPEARED IN MANY DIF-
FERENT FORMS TO MANY DIFFERENT PEOPLE AND YOU WERE
WRITTEN OF IN BOOKS, YOU WERE WRITTEN OF IN THE BOOK
OF MARK, YOU WERE WRITTEN OF IN *EITHER/OR* AND *MOUNT
ANALOGUE* AND *A VOID* AND MANY NAMELESS OTHER BOOKS,
YOU WERE WRITTEN OF IN LIBRARIES STUFFED FULL, YOU
WERE WRITTEN OF IN *ADVANCED SELLING FOR DUMMIES* AND
IN *PENTHOUSE* MAGAZINE, YOU APPEARED INSIDE SOFT TREES
IN A LOW LIGHT, IN EACH BOOK YOU MADE YOUR PRESENCE IN
SOME WAY, CAUGHT IN A BILLION MISSING LANGUAGES AND
IN EXPRESSIONS NOT YET DEFINED, EXPRESSIONS DEFINI-
TIONLESS AND UGLY AND UNPRONOUNCEABLE AND PROFANE.
IN THE WHITE REAM YOU WERE SOMEONE AND YOU WERE END-
LESS AND THERE WAS NOTHING YOU COULD NOT SAY. YOU
WERE NOT GOD.

The son leaned back in his desk chair. The son lit a cigarette he'd stolen from the father
and tried to think of something else. He thought about what he might have liked to eat for
dinner.

The reclining son was parallel to both the ceiling and the ground.

The messages' ringing in the room made the room pause.

    HELLO444: I CAN SEE U.

    HELLO444: I CAN SEE U.

    HELLO444: I CAN SEE U.

    HELLO444: I CAN SEE U.

    HELLO444: I CAN SEE U.

    HELLO444: I CAN SEE U.

The other person wrote it again and again and again.

The 45-year-old man was typing something also. The son did not look upon this message.
He continued typing to the other.

    [The Son]: who is this

    HELLO444: HOW ABOUT YOU TAKE A GUESS.

    [The Son]: mark

The son did not know a Mark.

HELLO444: NO. WRONG.

[The Son]: my father

HELLO444: GETTING WARMER.

HELLO444: NO.

The son thought about it, really. He felt something in his stomach.

[The Son]: my Friend from school.

He could not think of the girl's name or nicknames.

HELLO444: DINGDINGDING

[The Son]: hehe, yr weird

HELLO444: ☺.

HELLO444: WHO ELSE ARE YOU TALKING TO.

HELLO444: TALK TO ME, TALK TO ME ONLY.

The son looked at the screen. The son typed something then erased it. The son looked at the last few lines the 45-year-old man had typed, in which were described various difficult contortions of the son's body in the 45-year-old man's mind and the words, between them, they would say, *for our whole life*. The son touched his head.

[The Son]: so what r u up to

The small Friend did not answer.

[The Son]: sorry i am here now

[The Son]: ??

[The Son]: r u there

The son's cursor was blinking very fast. The son stared at the screen and drooled a little. The father's cigarette had burned down to his lip. The son closed the chat box window with the 45-year-old man and placed the man's screen name on his blocked list and deleted him from his friends on the social networking website and deleted his social networking profile and account and deleted all the emails to or from and saved direct chat logs with all the people in his archives who weren't the girl, his special friend.

The instant message box signaled that the girl was typing text. The son dug his nails into his flesh and waited. He heard the house around him sigh. He leaned and looked and leaned and leaned and leaned.

The last incoming message made no bell.

HELLO444: DO YOU WANT TO COME AND SPEND THE NIGHT AT MY HOUSE
ON THIS FRIDAY?

[The Son]: Y-E-S-S-S

INVERSE COLOR

The son could not find his cell phone. He'd been awaiting further word. The freezer had not become a tunnel as he'd been informed it would. The ceiling had not opened and the backyard had not learned to sing. The moon still seemed the same distance as always. Some of the son's hair had fallen out. The son thought about his father getting young instead of old. All of these things he'd been promised. The son pressed his teeth against his teeth. He got up and left the bedroom for the hall.

From the hall the son turned around and looked at the room where he'd just been. There was a wet spot in the bed where he had tried to sleep. As of the past few weeks the son could not wear a shirt without soaking through it, ruining the cloth. His sweat contained acidic properties. The son stunk often and a lot. While he was sick the son had hardly sweat at all. He couldn't urinate or cry. His eyes were itchy and black with pus. His body bloated with all the liquids the doctors forced on him to drink. His skin would grow distended and they'd

have to siphon off the excess through tubing that led to buckets that were carried somewhere away. The son heard something in the house behind him. He turned around to look. His brain moved quicker than his body. The room swam in long blond trails. As he turned, he saw his body moving down the hallway stairs. He was fairly certain it was his body. He had not often seen himself from behind, but his other self was wearing one of his favorite shirts—the shirt he had on when first entering the house. The son moved toward the stairs.

Passing the parents' bedroom, he heard the mother talking to herself in a language the son had only heard one time—heard through the crack in his old bed frame, the bed the men in plastic had come to haul away—the bed the doctors said had been infested and was the reason the son got sick. The son knew that wasn't why he'd gotten sick. It was a bed. No one would listen. The son had heard the mother's language noises once coming also from a crack in his newer bed but he'd stuffed the crack with gum. The house would sing to him for hours. The son did not try the parents' door.

The son had something crawling in his hair that was not of sufficient mass for him to feel.

The son came down the stairwell with his eyes crisscrossed in blur. They could not parse the light right for some reason. The son saw a haze across the landing. The son held the rail and breathed and breathed. There was a certain smell about the house now, as if someone was in the kitchen burning grease. He could hear some sort of conversation. The room composed around the son. The front door was standing open. In the dead bolt, there was a key. The key had no holes in it with which one could slide the key onto a loop or key chain. The key was large. The key burned the son's right hand. The son took the key and put it somewhere no one would find it.

The son walked into another room.

The son walked into another room, still looking, and another, larger room.

In each room the son heard movement moving in the room he'd just come from or ahead. In each room, he felt he'd just been in there. He could sense the grace of recent movement. Each little thing just out of place. The coffee-table magazines set out of order—magazines the son had never seen, affixed with dates still yet to come. The son could hear his cell phone ringing, though the tone seemed out of key. The son's phone's normal ringtone was from a song his mother had always sung to him inside her, though he only knew that because she said. The son couldn't remember where he'd left the cell phone. He couldn't tell from where the ring was ringing. It seemed all around. It seemed inside him. The son continued on. The lights in the room were going funny. The lights spun fluttered. The lights were off.

THE SON

Through one room the son had to go down on his knees to keep heading forward. At some point he had to stop and rest. The house was brighter when he looked again. The rooms were redder. There were several extra doors. The son kept turning and seeing things from a distance. The son kept repeating the same words. Sometimes the son would come into a room and swear he was coming into the room he'd just come into when coming into the current room from the one before, and sometimes the son would come into a room and swear he'd never seen the room inside the house at all, and sometimes the son would come and there would be nowhere else to walk, and the room would have no ins or outs or exits: windows, doors.

It took time before the son caught up with himself, there in the kitchen. In the window, he stood reflected. The son's reflection had his cell phone in his hand. The son stopped and watched him move. His motions did not quite match the ones that he was making. His

reflection was a little off-aimed, not quite there. For instance, as the son reached to touch his forehead, his reflection touched his neck. As the son opened his mouth in yawning, his reflection appeared to exhale. The son tried to say his name into him and the room went upside-down.

MIRRYRAMID

From work, by now, the father knew, there was not time enough to return home. His last trip there and back had required more than a quarter of a day—though really the father could no longer remember how long a day was these days—time was simply time. As soon as he pulled into his driveway, he'd have to turn around and head to work again. He hadn't even turned the car off, and still clocked in more than an hour late, an infraction for which his wages would be heavily penalized. He'd been so zoned then, that last time leaving, he'd not seen the black object on the neighbor's yard grown even larger, edging out into the street, so large you couldn't even see the neighbor's house behind it.

During this last drive he'd felt his eyes forcing themselves closed stuck on the highway, and for long distances with his eyes closed he drove and drove.

Days were weeks and weeks were days inside the father. At least that's what the banner

along the longest office hallway said, black text on white paint right outside his cubicle:

DAYS ARE WEEKS AND WEEKS ARE DAYS INSIDE YOU

Looking too long at the words' letters in relief would cause the father to go gooey—soft umbrellas in his thighs.

The father had never seen another body on his hallway, though he could hear them through the walls: typing, typing, breathing, eating, stuff.

God, he was hungry, the father realized, in third person. Tacos! Meat! Though there wasn't time enough to take a break now, the father knew. No, he had this box that gave the light out, which he must attend to, into which he also sometimes typed.

JOB

Each time the father hit a certain specific combination in cohesion with another input in the buildings' many cubicles and aisles, inside another room, on floors beneath the ground, a mouth set in a white flat wall spit out another black and gleaming box.

HOLE

In the front room, through the open door, the son saw how ants were coming in. The son thought he'd shut the door but it was open. The key was no longer in his hand. There were hundreds of ants, thousands of them, clustered in weird lines along the carpet, headed up the stairs—new crudded skeins of running cells—black—like glistened mobs of moving mold. They were everywhere, innumerable. They streaked in long neat lines up the house walls and into cracks riddled with holes. They made a buzzing sound like bees.

The son stood in the flood of influx with them swarmed around his legs. The son could not unfocus his attention. He was staring at his cell phone, which he'd taken from the other son. The handset had shifted color. It was gray now—gray as gross birds, birds which for weeks had flocked at the son's window, peering, chipping their whittled beaks on the long glass, wanting in, chirrup-chirrup-chirruping.

The son's phone had made 488 new outgoing calls in the last half hour. One specific number had been dialed 237 times. The son did not recognize the numbers. Some of the numbers did not have enough digits to be completed. Some of the numbers had digits that weren't digits. The phone had also received a handful of calls incoming but the numbers were in encoded scripts the son could not decipher. All of the numbers that had been stored in the son's phone—his mother's cell phone, the house number, his grandmother's house (the grandmother dead now and her number disconnected), 411 and 911, the number of the people who'd lived next door at the house they'd lived in before—where a little boy that looked a lot like the son had lived and he and the son had played together every day and the son had spoke into that child's head, giving into him the words he could create outside his body, overflowing from his silent book, until soon thereafter, in the spreading, the son got sick and swollen up and blue, bedridden, and then the neighbor was not allowed to see him and then they moved—all those familiar digits had been replaced with one single listing. It hurt the son's eyes to try to read the number. The phone's display was glowing very brightly.

The son stuttered upstairs toward the hall. The son crushed thousands at his feet. With each ant he crushed another thousand, each of them with eyes. All the eyes he crushed stuck to him, staying.

Certain of the stairs had been eaten through so completely the son felt his foot go through, sucked into the house.

The son felt sick. His eyes were spinning. The son bumped and fell against the wall, raining a sheath of loose ant matter off the drywall, off the layered phrase of paint, *each layer making the house that much smaller,* along the stretch of dry partitions, creating space, the

ants made veins toward the ceiling—webwork. The veins throbbed and fed the bodies into the overhead. The ants had ruined the hallway carpet, slurred in the fibers, drumming, gushed. They'd dug a rut around the bottom of the son's doorway, a series of smooth flat ridges gnawed—over which if breath were blown the right way, the fluted holes would give a sound. They'd moved the son's bed slightly to one side and seemed to be trying to flip it over. They crawled into drawers and across the mirrors and up more walls and across the ceiling, patterns. They'd congregated at a small hole that had been cut into the wall, thrumming from the crack into the bathroom. Their tiny backs were mirrored bubbles, glistening, bejeweled. The ants, in silence, programmed, at last there sharing the son's air.

ENTER

The son stood above the ants. The son stood watching. The son could not feel his fingers or his arms. The small reflective surface of each ant's head showed his head back into him, a chorus of him, gifted through the house. The son squeezed his phone so tight the skin in his arms and knuckles lost their blood. He could feel ants inside his organs, digging rings and ruts and lines. He could feel them eating in his lids, licking the color from his cornea and replacing it with something other, drummed, undone—something from inside the ants—something digested. The son could taste them in his mouth. He could feel them swimming in his bloodstreams, bathing. Through his colon. Threading his back. He could feel them in the center of his each tooth and hair stem. A black box building in his belly. The phone vibrating in his hands.

WHAT THE SON LEARNED THE ANTS HAD DONE

Downstairs the ants were in the TV—in the wires—in the nodes—as they had always been, in all homes. The ants were in the son. They'd etched their way into certain cushions, chewing room in for their den—they'd already formed a throne room—they'd made lengthy galleries and tombs—a nursery for the many coming newborn—the next time someone sat down on the sofa they would crush an empire and never know. The ants were in the son. The ants had crowned the son's image in the house in several portraits by eating holes into the paint around his head—they'd made rubbish of the inner workings of the simple lock in the son's doorknob—they'd covered every square inch of the son's bicycle—they'd nested slightly in his mattress—they'd kissed each other on the heads—they'd formed a necklace for several moments around the son's neck as he slept, which thereafter remained as rash—they'd gnawed a tunnel through the meat of certain books, the text around them chawed to mush. The ants were in the son. Other insects also had come in, though unlike the ants they hid in layers. They spun in futures. They knew the mindset of

a mold. Small white spiders small as pinheads hung jeweled along the ceiling of one room. The quilt the mother had been making for her one-day grandchildren—*the dream of other children always in her head*—had been ribboned through and through with mites. A flood of fluttered butterflies had collected on the velvet slide hung over the mantle, a wide piece of woolen fabric that had been in the house when the family moved in, and the family before them, and before them and on and on. The ants were in the son. From certain angles if you held your breath and asked a question, in the velvet you might see the profile of a man— though now the man's head was encrusted with chrysalis and soft wing gyration. Some certain kind of insect had laid its waste all through the foyer, the stink raising the temperature in the room by several degrees. Grasshoppers in the rice cooker. Roach babies in the sink. Wormy blankets burped by spiders—*enough to wrap your head*. Termites bundled in a jacket. Chiggers in the coffee grinds. Beetles in the grease and vents and elsewhere, waiting to awake. Insects so loud they could not be heard, obliterating words.

The father sat still in his small stall. The building's lights had been flickering for hours, a flat night club. Each direction seemed to go several directions. The more he worked the more there was.

I AM GOING TO LEAVE THIS ROOM NOW, the father typed into the machine.

THERE ARE OTHER THINGS I HAVE TO DO BESIDES TYPE INTO THE LIGHT.

I DON'T FEEL WELL AND THERE'S TROUBLE AND THESE DAYS AREN'T REALLY DAYS.

PLEASE LET ME BE   MORE OFTEN.

The cursor went on, silent beeping.

The father stood up, turned off the computer screen. He hesitated, glued. The way he was standing, the blank box looked straight on at his belly, an enormous glassy eye. It had such good warmth coming off it. The father rubbed his typing hands. At home, he knew, his wife and son were waiting, stuffed full of days that had just passed—days that as they accrued with those incoming would form wrinkles, pustules, new hair on their skin. These imperfections did not yet appear there in the older image of their faces hung on the wall above the father's desk—mother and son side by side there, smiling, in a room the father did not recognize. The father had not taken the picture, nor had he hung it there.

Beside the picture, sized just like it, a small square window in the building looked onto the outside. The window looked upon no other shore or building, but more light—the same color, grain, and sound of light as the machine's. Above the window, a small placard: *There is no year.*

The father grunted, made his hands fists. He swallowed on his spit, frothing suds between his cheeks in makeshift milkshake. He drank.

The father, feeling fatter, fuller, sat back down on his cube chair.

Into the black machine, with the screen off, the father typed as if he were at an organ, performing some small song.

INVERSE SOUND

And now the son had squeezed out all the toothpaste screaming.

And now a blurt had opened in the floor.

And now the room contained one billion windows.

And now the son felt sore.

And now the son felt his backbone shift slightly, pinching taut the skin around his cheeks
and lids.

And now the son moved to turn around inside the room and found he was too large to
turn around inside the walls.

And now the son felt his flesh compressed on all sides by something growing in and off the house.

And now the son could not stop coughing, and the tremor, and the ants.

And now the son was off the floor by inches and now the son's head compacted with his neck and his neck compacted with his ribcage and his ribcage puttered cream and the son felt his voice inside him slushed to zero and he felt his teeth grinding in his eyes and the son felt his bones becoming blubber and he felt the liquid in him brim.

And now the son spun around in one continuous direction, though from outside him he looked still.

And now the son's flesh could not contain his girth.

And now the son was more than tired and the son coughed up an enormous log of chalk and the son coughed up a pane of glass, a set of keys, and a door without a knob, and now the son's mouth sprayed out graffiti, the son gushed gold and gray and green, the son gushed glue and blue, and now the son coughed up a TV and now the TV screen was glowing and in the glow there someone stood and the house was shaking and made of money, and now the son coughed up a massive book, and the book began to read itself aloud into him, full of his words, and now the son would sing, and now the son coughed up a vein of hair he'd worn in styles of other years and the hair was drenched with grease he'd eaten and sugar he'd drunk and the hair wrapped around his head in coils, and now the son coughed up the sand of all the beaches and the heat of the son warped the sand down into glass, and through the glass the son saw other houses, and now the son coughed up wet and wax and coffee, and now the son coughed up more money by the sheet, and now

the son coughed a length of pipe, a bulb of moss, a flock of birds, a box inside a box, a travel guide with all blank pages, and now the son coughed up his sleep and now the son coughed up reams of endless skin still growing older and the son coughed up the son.

SKINNING

When the mother woke the following morning her body was as sore as it had ever been. In her sleep she'd drooled and sweated like the son and there the fluids had formed a kind of crust across her body and the bedsheets and the air. The mother's hair stuck to her cheek skin. The crust had spread across her eyelids and down her nostrils and in the grooving of her ears so that it took almost an hour with her nails digging as at blackboards before she could see well enough to cross the room.

In the bathroom the mother washed her face and body in the shower with the coldest water the house could make, holding her head against the pressure close with her mouth open, sucking spray. She could not seem to bring her mind and body out of sleeping. She could not quite bring her mind to think. The coldest water rinsed the mother and slicked bits off her body into the drain. The shower water exited the shower and the bathroom and the upstairs and the house. In its exit the shower water traveled deep into and through the

ground, met with other water that women and men within the neighborhood and others had used to clean or clear their bodies, water which would later be filtered and fertilized and redistributed on the earth—it would be mixed with bourbon in a dark room to help take the shaking out of a certain kind of man—it would be mixed with sugar and Kool-Aid powder at a young lady's seventh birthday party for the pleasure of the young lady and her seven guests, each of whom would bring a gift—it would be given to the sick to help with sickness. The water, via the mother and her others, would taste delicious. One day the water would return to rain.

While the mother dressed and did her hair and makeup—*even in sweat she kept a way*—she imagined a set of unseen hands lifting objects from rooms in the house. The mother had already begun packing the house up for moving in her mind. It hadn't been that long since they packed the last time. A certain percentage of the family's belongings were still boxed in the garage and attic—things the family did not need really except to help them remember who they'd been at other times—things that could have been removed and burned or melted down and the family would not have known the difference. Material of this nature comprised 62 percent of their belongings' mass. She imagined massive hands wrapping the beds and chairs and sofas in brown paper and sealing them with tape. She imagined the house lifted off the ground—brought to hover above the next house. She imagined the house turned on its side—the house turned fully over—its contents raining into place— the contents in the new house and the house made of years as yet to come, congealing and all else et cetera gone away. The family would be happy. They would

be happy. They would be happy. They would be happy. They would be happy. They would be happy. They would be happy.

They would be happy.

The mother could already taste the sweet indulgence of the low-fat imitation butter and sugar-free jam spread on the one-quarter wedge of a low-fat coupon-bought whole-wheat bagel that had been the mother's breakfast every morning for seven years. The mother worked her hand in circles of contentment across her belly, as she had while pregnant with the son.

The mother walked through the bedroom past the bed into the hallway and stopped. From the doorway in the hall there the mother could see into the son's room.

The son spread-eagled on the mattress, his hands clasped against his mouth—his thin arms stretched all taut through his pajamas emblazoned with shapes the mother had thought were Mickey Mouse heads when she bought them, though on closer examination she saw the ways the shape wavered from the popular icon into a thing she could not name—*and yet she let the son use them for sleep.* The son's torso seemed to have expanded—swollen perhaps, the mother thought first, reeling, with relapse, with new disease—though as she crossed the room she saw how the son had pulled on several layers for protection, as had she that other evening, every sweater that he owned, all ringed and hot and worn and chubby, the outermost sweater showing the son's name in neon puff-paint like the one the mother often wore, a pair of garments bearing their names, each, which had been given to them both at the same time, some occasion, though the mother could not think of who or what or when.

Around his neck the son had wrapped a scarf. Over his head he had a ski mask. Around

his feet he'd wrapped old T-shirts and on his hands he had baseball gloves, one turned the wrong way to fit the thumb. The fabric on the son's hands and legs was smeared with something runny. The son's hands clutched a shovel. The son didn't answer when she shook him. She found dirt nuzzled in his clothes. She stripped him clean layer by layer, like peeling some huge orange. The son was not opening his eyes. The mother said the son's name—again, again—her voice all flat. The son's skin was stretched and splotched in spots as it had been most of his sick year—a year now carried in the mother's flesh memory as a tiny colored lesion, one polka dot.

This child. This child. This child here. The mother inhaled and touched the son. She touched the son again a different way and said the son's name and touched her forehead. She spread her arms and said the name and held the son and kissed his fingers and tried to sing the song she'd always sung—a song she'd dreamt up when the son was still inside her, a song she used to calm their blood—though now she could not quite hear it—she could not think of all the words.

IN A DAZE THE SON REMEMBERS THE BLACK PACKAGE HE'D UP TILL NOW IGNORED OR FORGOTTEN OR SOMEHOW JUST NOT SEEN

The son lay in his bed. The mother downstairs, the mother having coaxed the son to waking, having held and wished and prayed above him until the son opened up his eyes.

The son had told the mother about the ants. He said it over and again until finally she'd lifted him up and led him through the house to see how all was well, nothing was there, not a thing, no ants. Not even one. Nor inside him, she said. Never.

Again alone, around the son the air was clear.

Alone the son lay cocked still and looking up, transfixed with something there above him, in his thoughts—*breath burnt like scratched black barns in yards of long grass smudged and smoldered—the son crimped and creaming—the son as a thing not in the room but of it—the son as a field of cells—the son—the son's backbone—the son's miles of intestine, fat with grease and shit and knitting—*

The son stopped thinking for a second and when the breath inside him broke he swung, sat up.

The son heard something near him moving. The lights inside the room were on.

The son moved and put his feet down. He turned around and saw behind him where ants were still there coming right in through the wall—through cracks, in hordes of slow procession from the bathroom to the closet where they'd gather in a mass. The son sneezed. He smiled. The ants. He'd said it. His mother did not know.

The son rose up from his chair and crossed the room.

The son moved into the closet with the ants beneath him and stood and looked among his stuff—the leagues of old dolls he'd once collected against his father's will, with sets of eyes each, the outgrown clothes, the many knives, the clippings of local outbreak he'd collected since his own sick, spread on the air—sick that since had kept a certain air about him, dirt and pickles—as well the snips he'd taken from his hair in private for safekeeping, *as had the father*, stashed in little baggies marked with dates—so much the son had stowed, not knowing.

The ants were not after these things.

The ants were swarming the black package.

They were all around it.

Mashing. Massive.

Clicking eyes.

Click clack.

The son had had the package in the closet all this time.

The son had stepped over it naked, getting dressed.

The box had seen his dick.

He'd walked around it like something that'd been affixed for ages, something built into the house and in the son's life—common as a keyhole or an eye.

The ants were all around the box. The son could hardly see. He could hardly remember where it'd come from.

He could not remember.

With the flat skin of his small hands, the son
brushed ants' bodies from the box.

At his touch the ants seemed
to die or stiffen or go dumb, slough-
ing off the box in crippled hordes.

The son lifted the box against his body and carried it back into his room.

In the exact center of the carpet he held the box between his knees.

The box's outer lining was a silky, stretchy putty that would not quite come off with his nails. The son stretched the stuff in strands of sheeting, slurring his cuticles, stuck deep. It burned.

The son went to the closet, hearing nothing. The son got out exactly the right knife.

There were no markings on
the outside of the package
except for two small
watermarks the son could not
see.

Under the black lining was another lining.

Under that lining was a box.

The box was a cloth-wrapped package, blackened, and kind of smashed along the sides. The addressee's name had been removed. The son split the seam edge on this new box with another certain kind of knife. He opened this new box as well and found inside it yet another. This next box was bubble-wrapped and wound around with tape. This box had a new address that had also been marked out.

When the son shook the package he could hear something in it move.

In the third package was another package.

In the fourth package was another package.

And the fifth, the sixth, the seventh.

What came out

194

of the seventh package seemed too large to have fit inside the others. It was nearly four times the size of even the original black package. It was writ with words, which ants were still swarmed over, crawling up the son's arms and in his armpits and his teeth.

Across the street, the **enormous box** upon the neighbor's yard—a mirror image of this seventh box, here—was changing shape.

The son had a tattoo now on his back. The
tattoo was of a tree. It discolored the son's
already discolored skin. The tree's branches
spread up his shoulders, up his neck toward
his eyes.

As the son unwrapped the center of
the seventh box the tattoo sunk into
another layer.

The son was
made of
layers, too.

In the seventh box's single center—fat and **bloodred**—there was a nodule.

The nodule had a lever.

The son pulled the lever
and the center bloomed—bloomed out into a
light—a light as large as many rooms—

—& the son
could not stop
shaking.

He could not stop.

???EGAKCAP EHT EDISNI SAW TAHW

Something wrapped in matte white paper.

Paper had no seam or sealant. Paper tasted clean.

The son scratched the paper with another knife till

there was room to use his fingers.

Inside the paper there was another box—

the son was getting tired

—a black box just like the first of all—

exactly the same box.

Inside the box,

inside more paper,

the son found a photo of

himself.

In the photo, the son was

older than he was now,

but the son could still

see that it was he. The

son had his mother's

eyes.

The photo was an 8" × 10" headshot printed on photographic paper. The son's autograph appeared at a slight angle across the gloss. The son's autograph touched the divot in his image's Adam's apple. The son could not tell if his autograph was actual or stamped on. The son traced his autograph with his ring finger. Then he could no longer feel his arm.

The son's photo was the first of many photos stacked together in a pile.

The son shuffled through the pictures in the pile one after another, placing each thereafter on the bottom of the stack.

Bas Jan Ader,[27]

Joan of Arc,[28]

Kaspar Hauser,[29]

Egon Schiele,[30]

Bruce Lee,[31]

Brandon Lee,[32]

Tim Buckley,[33]

Jeff Buckley,[34]

Malcolm X,[35]

Pier Paolo Pasolini,[36]

Ann Quin,[37]

---

27 Bas Jan Ader died lost at sea while attempting to cross the Atlantic alone in performance of a piece he titled *In Search of the Miraculous*.

28 Joan of Arc died by fire and then was burned twice again, to ashes, to prevent the preservation of relics of her flesh.

29 Kaspar Hauser died of a stab wound inflicted on him by a stranger who also handed him a small bag containing a message written backward.

30 Egon Schiele died three days after his wife and spent the time between their deaths drawing sketches of her.

31 Bruce Lee died with his brain having swollen by 13 percent.

32 Brandon Lee died on a film set almost exactly twenty years after his father.

33 Tim Buckley died as a result of his response to the direct challenge "Go ahead, take it all."

34 Jeff Buckley died in a river almost exactly twenty-two years after his father.

35 El-Hajj Malik El-Shabazz died in sunlight standing before a crowd of more than four hundred.

36 Pier Paolo Pasolini died on a beach that often appeared in his novels, after being run over several times by his own car.

37 Ann Quin died while swimming out to sea.

Wesley Willis,[16]

Marc Bolan,[17]

Bobby Darin,[18]

Charlie Parker,[19]

Tupac Shakur,[20]

Ol' Dirty Bastard,[21]

Simone Weil,[22]

William Burroughs Jr.,[23]

Srinivasa Ramanujan,[24]

Ian Curtis,[25]

Aubrey Beardsley,[26]

---

16 Wesley Willis died having recorded more than a thousand songs.

17 Marc Bolan died leaving a supposed curse on those he'd known, which thereafter has been associated with more than a dozen incidents of premature death.

18 Bobby Darin died of blood poisoning from dental medication despite eight hours on the operating table.

19 Charlie Parker died inside a body mistaken by his coroner to be twenty years older than it actually was.

20 Tupac Shakur died as a result of gunshot complications after spending six days in a medically induced coma, and posthumously continued to release albums.

21 Russell Jones died with a doubled plastic bag of narcotics hidden in his stomach.

22 Simone Weil died refusing to eat more than small amounts of food, opening her body to her disease.

23 William Burroughs Jr. died having returned to the state where he was raised in search of help.

24 Srinivasa Ramanujan died after being incorrectly diagnosed and thus not receiving treatment for his infection, which could have easily been cured.

25 Ian Curtis died after watching Werner Herzog's *Stroszek* and listening to Iggy Pop's *The Idiot*.

26 Aubrey Beardsley died very early in the morning on a hotel bed sometime after having begged his publisher to destroy his obscene work.

In the pile there were photos of

Antonin Artaud,[1]

Sharon Tate,[2]

Andy Kaufman[3]

&

Heather O'Rourke.[4]

The son recognized these first four from a film he'd seen somewhere, though he could not
remember where or when.

---

1 Antonin Artaud died alone, seated at the foot of his bed, holding his shoe.

2 Sharon Tate died tied neck to neck with another person while thirty-four weeks pregnant.

3 Andy Kaufman died leaving the premonition in several others that he hadn't.

4 Heather O'Rourke died soon after completing a trilogy of films about a cursed family, after which several
other members of the cast are said to have also died prematurely.

In the pile there were photos of

Chris Farley,[5]

Heath Ledger,[6]

Krissy Taylor,[7]

River Phoenix,[8]

Bill Hicks,[9]

Cliff Burton,[10]

Christa McAuliffe,[11]

DJ Screw,[12]

Timmy Taylor,[13]

Flannery O'Connor,[14]

Wolfgang Amadeus Mozart,[15]

---

5 Chris Farley died wearing sweatpants and an open button-down shirt.

6 Heath Ledger died lying facedown on a bed.

7 Krissy Taylor died despite more than an hour of attempted resuscitation.

8 River Phoenix died after falling on the ground and convulsing for eight minutes.

9 Bill Hicks died twelve days after ceasing speaking in his parents' home in Little Rock, Arkansas.

10 Cliff Burton died after winning the right to the bed he died in by pulling the ace of spades from a deck of cards.

11 Christa McAuliffe died attempting to enter outer space.

12 Robert Earl Davis Jr. died on the floor of the bathroom of his recording studio after his fifth heart attack, chemically induced.

13 Timmy Taylor died in a one-car accident on the way home from a recording session during the production of his band's major-label debut.

14 Flannery O'Connor died thirty-three years before her mother.

15 Johannes Chrysostomus Wolfgangus Theophilus Mozart died and was buried in a common grave with no mourners in attendance.

John Belushi,[38]

Jean-Michel Basquiat,[39]

Jonathan Brandis,[40]

Keith Moon,[41]

Rainer Werner Fassbinder[42]

&

David Foster Wallace.[43]

Photos near the bottom of the pile contained people the son had never heard of. Some were named with names that didn't even sound like normal human names. Some were dressed in obscure clothing and yet still wore tasteful makeup and a photogenic expression. Some of the photographs appeared to have been ripped or shredded and then taped back together or laminated. The son's fingers did not leave prints along the gloss.

---

38 John Belushi died having recently filmed a cameo in which he was portrayed facedown in a swimming pool, dead.

39 Jean-Michel Basquiat died having hid many of his best works to keep them from being sold.

40 Jonathan Brandis died after his performance in one of his last roles was cut from the film.

41 Keith Moon died a few weeks after the release of the album *Who Are You*, on the cover of which he appears seated backward on a chair to hide his weight gain.

42 Rainer Werner Fassbinder died with a cigarette in his mouth and blood pouring from one nostril.

43 David Foster Wallace died with a massive and uncompleted manuscript found bathed under light in his garage.

The son held the pictures looking at them. The son felt his arms make paste.

The son felt nauseated trying to move past certain pictures. Some pictures caused sores to open on the son's head.

The son could not stop
looking yet.

The people in the pictures
did not blink.

The son felt a tone
sound through his ster-
num.

The son's belly button
sealed over.

The son shifted the pile again so that his photo sat on top.

The son looked at the son again.

The son put the photos down.

The son was buzzing in his knees a little.

The son's top and bottom teeth had singed together.

The son was mostly on the ground.

Also from the
box there with
the photos the
son pulled out
a small black
coil.

The coil had
an outer layer,
with a thread
clasp.

The coil
unfurled to
become a long
black bag—a
black bag
made of
leather and
about the size
of an XXXL
nightgown, or
a balloon.

The bag held
its mouth
closed with a
metal zipper.

The son
unzipped the
zip.

He held his
face up to the
bag and
looked in.

There was
nothing in the
bag.

No smell,
no light,
no hour.

The son
emphatically
inhaled.

The son
touched
the bag
against
his
forehead.

The son
kissed
the bag.

THREE

I never told a joke in my life.

ANDY KAUFMAN

RENEGE

Within the duration of one hour on the nose in the long corralled light of afternoon, the mother received a phone call from every agent and buyer who'd submitted offers on the house. Each retracted in soft formal English as if their words had been lifted from a manual. Each hung up the phone before the mother spoke. One man said, I am exhausted and can no longer feel my hands, though he sounded rather chipper. At the end of that one hour, the couple's agent also called—a man who sounded most exactly like the man himself, except for the manner by which he chewed. The couple weren't retracting their offer, the agent assured the mother, as she began to weep into the phone. There was the sound of something plastic closing or coming open. The agent stated their new claim: the couple was now offering a sum of $19,000 for the real estate—almost a 90 percent drop from the original offer—which was to be paid directly from buyer to seller in a series of biannual installments equaling a certain modest percentage of the remainder outstanding on the house. The agent acknowledged—at the mother's prodding—how such a payment plan

would never actually get the house paid off. Instead, an endless minor diminishing toward zero, a payment scheduled to be terminated after both the father and the mother's passing. The couple was not willing to involve third parties such as a moneylender or the like, the agent explained, as they were private with their ways of living and to get a loan you had to tell a lot of people a lot of shit. The agent actually said the word *shit* into the phone hotly, using a tone laden with some strange amount of venom and, no doubt, spittle, at which point the mother terminated the call. When the phone began to ring again immediately, she took the phone off the hook and left it that way for the remainder of the day, so that whatever sounds the house or family made were broadcast to an open line.

REDRESS

The mother spent the next several hours with her head against a wall. She tried to push with sufficient force to make her face join with the house. Instead she learned to smile a little wider. In the backyard she could hear what seemed a hundred screeching, squealing dogs and car alarms. Some people singing, maybe. An implosion. The mother went to the window and saw nothing but bright light. The mother stared into the light until her pupils zeroed, until even when she turned her head the room was washed. Washed. Worked white, dewormed.

Seeing white, the mother put herself to work. She began first mopping the kitchen, sloshing soap across the blinded tile. In other rooms she grunted on her knees with brush and carpet soap, stench expanding in her head. She washed the floors in every room the house had. In certain rooms the mother found infestation. Not *leagues* of ants, the way the son had said, but little trickles invading through small cracks, creating grainy graded torrents and tiny turrets. The ants crumpled on contact, tidal, their tiny bodies sloshed in venom.

Closer up, the mother found, pinching one's thorax between her two longest fingers, these were not ants but something else. They had a different shape of head and tiny patterns on their bellies, which almost looked like words. The mother swept the tiny carcasses into a dustbin with one gloved hand. She cured the sodden carpet on her hands and knees with the hairdryer and combed away the smell. She did not want the son to know.

In the son's bathroom, where she'd not been since the sales show, the mother came to stand before the hole in the wall between the bathroom and the son's room where the veiled woman had cut through. In the gap between two walls, she discovered, a thick clear gel had been stuffed into the air—had been stuffed, or always been there—always in the house. An odd shade for insulation, she imagined. Plus it was cold and had a throaty smell, like chowder.

Through the hole the mother could see into the son's room from a new angle, to the bed. The room looked differently from this perspective: smaller, taller. She could not see the other door, though it should have been right there on the wall cattycorner. On the bed, a mirror facing face-up, toward the ceiling, its surface bending slightly in.

The mother walked from the hole back through the bathroom to the son's door set on the hall. The door had been left wide open. The son was not there in the bed. There was no hole there where the hole was, from the bathroom—there instead, the mirror hung. She closed the door behind her, nodded. There were two rooms.

The mother closed her eyes. She walked back into the bathroom feeling her way. Back at the rip there, the hole, the pucker, the mother worked with eyes still closed. The mother spread the wall with putty over the new hole, sealing it full whole. The first few blobs went hot and runny and sank into the surface. It burned her on the hands. She had to reapply the

substance several times before it stuck and even then it slid and bubbled. She sang inside her, making silence, rehearsing lines from a play she'd been in the year just before the child was born—lines sealed inside herself. When the new wall was halfway dry the mother pressed her thumb into its softish face. The mother felt something transfer through her.

The mother went back into the house and washed the floors again. She washed the floors again. She washed the floors until she could crawl upon them. Until she could lick and kiss and laugh and feel fine in this house clean of all others. She could somehow hear the mirror, upstairs, shaking.

Yes yes yes, the mother said, rolling. Yes yes yes yes yes yes yes yes yes yes yes yes yes yes.

Now with the momentum really in her, gassed and ticking, the mother drove to the grocery down the street and bought as much cleaning product as she could carry. All the prices seemed very high. She watched the items scan across an electronic neon zapper by a young man who would not open his mouth or blink his eyes. *The young man had a photograph in his pocket, folded halfway fourteen times, a picture of himself contorted in a position that made his body seem to not be there.* The mother handed this young man her cash. He looked, too, like the young father, though the mother could not remember who that was.

Back at home the mother took the son out on the battered lawn to sit and gather sun. She'd called again to keep the child home, nearer to her, needing. The mother felt determined. Her insides goggled, warm with war. There was nothing about the house she'd leave to fester any longer. The mother wrapped a clean dry cloth around her face and forehead, leaving room only for her eyes. She patrolled the house wielding one can after another, spraying every surface, every inch. She wiped and foamed and sprayed and swished and

swum and wiped. She cleaned the walls, the floors (again), the blades of fans, the blades of knives and other utensils, the countertops, air vents, knobs and handles, baseboards, corners, nooks, books (she thumbed through pages), closets, clasps, curtains, windows, boxes, things inside boxes, crumbs in cracks. She stood on stools on chairs on tiptoes and splashed the ceiling down. Her body sizzled lightly. Her fingers tingled from how they weren't getting enough blood.

Outside the house took on an aura. The chemic stink pillowed out for blocks. The mother went out and strapped the son's face with its own mask. She still felt she had not done enough. She felt impulsive. She went back through the house, now walking backward. She began to take certain things against her chest. She smashed ceramic heirloom plates. She took the street numbers off the house. She called the phone company and had their number changed. She took the bed linens and pillows into the backyard and burned them. She burned the picture of the man and of the father at the party. She burned some clothing. She burned a sofa. She burned the relics of the son's condition. It was time. The past. The after. The mother felt she had been foolish. Caught up. She burned the plaster cast of the son's chest and his sick drawings and his thermometers, his night-light. She burned any inch that had held ill.

The mother thought of other things to do. In the half-light of the bugged sun, the mother went through the woods wielding a steak knife, in search of the place she'd hid the copy son but she could not find him among all else. She dragged the winter lid onto the pool.

The mother's mind designed itself.

By the end of early evening, the house felt mostly new. If not new, clean. If not clean, better. If not better, something. The mother snuck one of the father's cigarettes from underneath his pillow. She went behind the house to smoke it, watching the son from around the

corner of the house. The light over the house seemed like something funneled through a tarp. The air was thick and rather fat. The son was smiling. He had strange teeth—chalked and spattered with flecks of diseased color. The son might never kiss a woman. The son did not like to kiss regardless. The mother stroked her arm a little. The mother dragged the last ash from the cig and tabbed the butt against her whitish tongue and pressed her tongue against the mouth roof and sucked a little with saliva and chewed and choked it down. She felt it nuzzle in her stomach. She watched the son and smoked again.

GAME

The son.

The son was in the TV room. The room was there still, in the house, its carpet's color matching the chafe marks on his knees. The father and the mother were upstairs talking in voices the son could hear bleed through vents, ballooning. The son was sitting on the sofa in the center of a stain. A stain that had not been there when he sat down. A stain that matched another stain made somewhere else.

That morning the son had found his old video game system in the box beneath his bed—a thing he hadn't used in years, a portal to old worlds defined by pixel, light, and color. For certain months of a certain year certain men had sat in certain rooms and typed on keyboards creating language that would then be stored and replicated on the plastic cartridges such as the one the son now had employed. This language fed into the son via his open undone eyes. The son was pressing buttons.

In the game the son was represented by a figure. The son could cause the figure to move in one direction or another. The son could lead the figure to die. The son's small fingers were fat with callus from where he'd spent countless hours in this system. The son could burn the pad of his left index finger with a lighter for several minutes and still not feel a thing. Certain sections of the game the son knew so well he could close his eyes and still complete them.

The son.

The son had groove marks in his armpits and around his shoulders and in his hair from where the ants had dug into him, where they'd searched for a way in, where they'd bit. The son would never know how much he'd bled. The son could have filled a shopping mall with platelets.

The son pressed the button that made the figure jump across the chasm. The son watched the sky above the figure become riddled with explosion, swathed with gray and green and yellow bits and blocks.

In the front face of the plastic game console there were three other outlets where three other players could plug in and control their own figure, but those three other outlets remained unfilled: three more eyes. The son watched the time allotted to complete some current objective ticking in increments toward zero. There was so much going on.

The son watched the figure fall through a section of block he'd believed stable, but in fact held nothing there. The figure fell down a lengthy corridor just wide enough to fit the figure's breadth. The son had never seen this happen. The son had played and beat the game many, many times, had read magazines relaying the secrets the game contained, the un-

locking patterns pressed by many thousands of other players playing the same version of this same game, the son had done it all, and yet he had not seen this. The sound the game made seemed to clip in and out.

The room the figure fell into was made of walls. There was nothing much about them. The walls went on and on. There was nothing for the son to make the man jump over. There were no balls of fire or enormous rabbits, no floating crystal that squirted liquid, and no moving splotch with eyes. The room was just a room. An endless room in one direction. And yet the son could not get more than a certain distance through the level. He kept dying, getting zapped or smeared or squashed. Most of the time he did not know what caused the zapping, smearing, squashing—it came from nowhere. He tried again and again and the game let him keep choosing to endlessly continue, whereas usually once you died a certain number of times you had to start over. Each time the son continued he reappeared inside the same unending room.

The son played the level for several hours, still not getting any further. The game's music kept on with one corrupted tone that seemed to pan back and forth inside the son's head. Sometimes there were little torches or bitmapped symbols that showed the figure was moving forward. The son had not eaten food and swallowed water at any point throughout the day—*this was in the game's design.* The son made the figure do things to try to find a glitch inside the level. The son made the figure throw himself into the ceiling. The son made the figure duck down and up and down and up in patterns. He made the figure stand and squat and stand and squat and walk endlessly forward into a wall into which no matter how hard the son pressed the buttons he could not force the figure through.

The son stopped pressing buttons for a minute and looked at the screen. The son felt frustrated. He felt something click inside his boredom. The son pressed a series of many but-

tons into the control pad with his thumbs. He pressed the buttons in an order that was not intentional but still came out of him himself.

The sequence formed by the son's button pressing caused a small black square across the screen. The black square covered over a certain section of the long room's pixelated ceiling, around which the other pixels went slurred and glitchy. The son's current score appeared deformed, though he could still read the last six digits, all still zeroes.

Something in the room around the son released an air. The figure representing the son inside the game went locked. No matter what buttons the son would press now the figure would not respond. The son pressed more buttons, feeling angry. He rapped his knuckles on the screen. Inside, briefly, he heard something knocking back. The TV began to hum. The screen felt warm—too warm. The son was looking at the figure. Above, the square spread rapidly across the screen, aiming to cover over all. The son saw the figure begin to wriggle. The figure turned his head toward the son. The figure was looking at the son now most directly and there was something written in his eyes—something carried in the figure all those hours—carried over in every replicated instance of his entire life

Inside the game the music paused out, nowhere. The figure's mouth fell open, in an O.

Along the bottom of the screen, a scrolling text, each instance beeping:

Help

Help

Help

Help

Help

Help

Help

227

SURROUND

In his car along the street among the houses in the light—something shaking where the sun was—*some complex hole*—the father could not remember how to get to home. He was supposed to be already back at his desk now for the next day, for more staring. He could not even feel the wheel.

He sent an email from his cell phone to his superior, a man he'd never seen or heard or known by name:

> *To Whom It May Concern:*
>
> *Sick. Sorry. Soon.*
>
> *Yours,*

A reply came back in several seconds.

To Whom It Does Concern:

You snide shit. I'm getting groggy. I am becoming an ex-
ploder and you are nearby. I have sleds in my sheep barn—
barn, barn, house, your house. Got it? Suck one. Suck
good. And bring an extra arm.

Best,

Somewhere now out lost in loops around the building—*where was the building?*—the father could not at all recall even the direction he'd made the car aim in the name of home all those evenings, and those mornings, in reverse—which way to go now in the nowhere that had settled on the air. Today the day was bruisy like a dropped baby and half of the sky seemed stood before, as if by god, or a cardboard cutout of god in god's absence, wherever he or she or it had gone. The father refused to capitalize the word god even inside his mind, despite how in the night inside his mind when he could not sleep, he prayed. Prayed so loud inside his mind it hurt, it made the house stink, which his wife assumed was indigestion.

Inside the car the father rolled long along the street among the buildings in the light— something shaking where the sun was—*he'd already thought all this before.* His balding head was pounding. The streets and trees had blanched a white. Where there'd been strip malls somewhere before, billboards, the wet and wire were all covered in a gloss, webbed fat with chrysalis or kite-string—an ever-present mayonnaise. By miles the roads would loop back to where they started, farting the father back out nowhere clear. The nearest

roads' names had changed to SLORISISIIISSISS, VORDBEND, MONNNNNEY. There was nowhere clear to get a beer.

Along the streets in all directions a slow, thick rain raining in rising from the earth into the sky.

Inside his car the father felt an awful feeling there was something breathing besides him. Something right there on the backseat, strapped in, needing, shaped like him. He could not bring himself to peek. Through the windshield in his car out in the street among the houses in the light the father watched the car continue forward, scrolling, returning where he'd been again already—no sound—the years inside him itching, eating, and, outside, the years upon him soon to come.

INFINITE REFLECTION

In the night the son stood in the bedroom as the sun outside was coming down. Its orb slid from the sky in staggered increments, leaving a slight residue behind in slur, and where it began. The face of the sun itself was ragged and discolored, swimming—a humming hole impenetrable to eye. The way the light came through the window made the bedroom slow, the glass reflective, holding night out and inside in.

Parallel to there, just at his second side, the son had set the mirror on the air. He posed his body at an angle catching himself there in the two quick flattened planes reflected back and forth between the glass and glass a billion times, his body, each with mouth and skin and headholes replicated till there were more of him than he could stand. All of him crowded in and shouting: a maze of sons under no sun. Bruised skin in a relief map. Buttons.

LOOK AGAIN

In the room below the son's room the windows had gone tinted. The son had taken the video game console and put it in the trash compactor but it would not break. He'd put the mirror in the compactor and it had shattered, but when he went back upstairs there it was again.

The son stripped nude and got in bed, the wood frame groaning. He ran his fingers along his bruises. The skin there rumpled, rain-run, discolored, something beneath. The son chewed on the divots in his forearm: piano noise. He could taste it coming off in sheeting. His legs would not stay still. His brain would not go quiet. What if he'd been born several seconds later? What if he'd been born under another name? What if on the thirty-fifth day the mother was pregnant the mother had shone a flashlight down her throat; or read the Bible backward; or heard some certain song; or pressed her cheek against a saw?

The son's flesh rolled between his small hands, doughy. He felt something spark between his teeth and there inside them. A little liquid dripped down from his ears. He heard a whirring in his stomach like garage doors. The whole room seemed to squeeze. The son was tired. He was talking to himself. The room seemed to flutter in his eyelids, eyes behind them. The walls would lean or move. The carpet grew long. There was a boulder rolling above the bed. There were eyes on every surface. There was someone in the mattress.

The son saw the bedroom door come open. The door moved forward on its hinges just a crack. The son closed his eyes, pretending. He heard someone move into the room. He did not want to look. He did not look.

The son's flesh rolled between his small hands, doughy. He felt something spark between his teeth and there inside them. A little liquid dripped down from his ears. He heard a whirring in his stomach like garage doors. The whole room seemed to squeeze. The son was tired. He was talking to himself. The room seemed to flutter in his eyelids, eyes behind them. The walls would lean or move. The carpet grew long. There was a boulder rolling above the bed. There were eyes on every surface. There was someone in the mattress.

The son saw the bedroom door come open. The door moved forward on its hinges just a crack. The son closed his eyes, pretending. He heard someone move into the room. He did not want to look. He did not look.

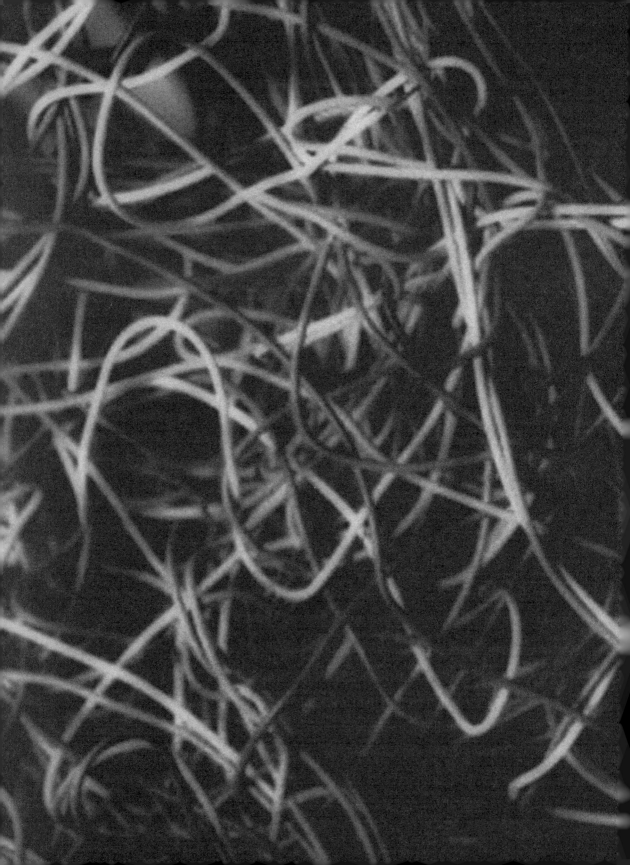

INDICATIONS OF THE MANNER BY WHICH YOU WILL ARRIVE

The son received directions to the girl's house in a black envelope delivered in the night. There'd been no one in the hallway. The son had not slept. He hadn't seen the girl at school since the invitation. None of the teachers knew a thing. The other students still would not acknowledge him. The girl's locker seemed to be filled with some kind of buzz. The girl's directions were several pages long and writ in ink that changed colors in the light. The son read them again and again, over and over until he could hear them in his head:

FIND AN EGG—ANY EGG!—BREAK THE EGG OPEN—IN THE EGG THERE IS A KEY—WRAP THE KEY INSIDE A TUFT OF HAIR THEN PLACE IT ON YOUR TONGUE—NOW SUCK!—GO THROUGH THE INSIDE TO THE OUTSIDE— TAKE A RIGHT—A RIGHT—A LEFT—A SLIGHT RIGHT—A RIGHT—YOUR OTHER RIGHT—A RIGHT AGAIN—GOOD JOB—IF AT ANY POINT YOU PASS A **LIBRARY**,

TAKE A KNEE & BURN YOUR FINGER WITH A MATCH—NOW OUTSIDE A PIC-
TURE WINDOW WITH NO PICTURE CURL ON THE GROUND INTO A BALL—ROLL
FORWARD ONCE FOR EACH TIME YOU'VE KISSED YOUR MOTHER—FOR EACH
TIME YOU'VE GIGGLED, MARK YOUR ARM—RECITE THE WITNESS—CALL THE
NUMBER—SPIT THE KEY INTO THE SAND—THE KEY WILL SINK—DIG AFTER
THE KEY WITH YOUR LONGER FINGER—WHEN YOU FIND THE KEY AGAIN YOU
WILL HAVE FOUND A WALL—THE WALL WILL OPEN—LET THE SAND FILL IN
BEHIND YOU—COME IN ALONE—I WILL BE THERE SHORTLY—NO ONE MUST
KNOW—NO ONE MUST KNOW—GO.

The directions continued on for pages, including footnotes. There was a map so splotched
with lines and symbols you could not see through it even when you held it up to the light.

The son sent the girl an email—*LOL, say wha?* The girl did not respond. The son did not
know the girl's last name to look it up. The son felt much too warm.

And yet when it came time to go, he went. He didn't tell the father or the mother where he
was going, as he knew the mother would not let him—not alone.

That night the son shaved his face for the first time with a knife he found inside his hand when
he woke up. He did not notice all the blood, or the strange smell, or the nodule in his hair.

The son was an expert at forgetting.

EXIT METHOD

The son walked into the long night. He went up one street and down another. He turned and turned at times for turning. The streetlamps were dead or blue or strobed. The trees along the roadside hung down right against the gravel, fat with slug and chrysalis, thick with ash. The son walked. The son crawled a little. The son's legs began to ache. The son tried to hail a long white taxi that barreled past him but the taxi did not slow or stop. Through the taxi windows the son saw no one. The son felt hungry. His hair was itching. The son licked his wrists. The son looked into the light. The night was scorched and streaked in lines. The son could hardly see. The son's pants were wet around the edges, though it hadn't rained in months. The son got a nosebleed. His skin felt heavy. There were wrinkles in his face. The son took a minute to lie down—an exit method he'd grown fond of—and against the earth his body rattled. The dirt was hard and itching, filled with lumps that bulged and warmed and wormed. The son rolled into some grassing. The grass smelled familiar. The son nodded off. The son woke up and walked. He saw the sky above him. The sky was gush-

ing green. The sky was wrapped in mosses attached to trees attached to houses. There was a constellation in the shape of a dead horse. The son walked underneath it. A flood of pigs ran past. One of the pigs was a man on hands and knees. A pack of long dogs with even longer ass hair came after. The son no longer wished to go where he was going. He had never felt so tired. The son turned to head back the way he'd come but everything behind him now looked different. The concrete was bright yellow and glowed inside its cracks. Sometimes the cracks ejected worms. A man came out of the dark and asked the son for a quarter. The son said he didn't have any money. The man asked again and the man asked. The man tried to touch the son's face and the son began to shake and the son said I swear I don't have any money. The son pulled out both pockets to prove it and out of the son's pockets change came falling. It fell all across the floor—the outside had a floor now, made of vinyl mashed and melted down from all the records ever, reflective, clean—and the man fell down onto the money and hoarded it into his mouth with both hands and with his mouth overflowing the man's voice came out, and the man said, I knew that you were a liar, you've always been a liar, always will be, that's what you are, and the son could hear the money rubbing on the man's tongue and his own tongue and he could taste it melting in his cheeks, the metal money filled his mouth so much he could not find a way to speak, and the man was rolling on the ground beside him in the money and the man was coughing out one long endless sound and the man looked exactly like the man the son had seen inside his mother's mother's locket and he looked exactly like the man who'd been only a head, the man who'd touched the sickness in him, the man was chewing on the money so hard he was chewing his own face and the man's face was bleeding and the face unfolded and the man's eyes split apart, and the man had five eyes, eight, ten, thirty gleaming, thirty thousand, a thousand thousand, and then the man had no eyes at all and the son felt frightened and the son turned to run and as he ran his hair grew out behind him long and rippled, fat with wind, and the son's hair began to try to tie itself to things such as the man's hair and the vinyl and the sky now burping overhead and the hair was pulling the son back down in

anger and the son felt his cell phone ringing and the son took his phone out and answered and inside the phone someone was screaming and the son hung up the phone and tried to call his mother but the phone would not pick up a signal and the phone kept beeping through its speaker and someone was trying to call him back and the son could not get the phone off of his face again and his skin was sticking to his hair and fingers and the son ran and ran and ran and ran and ran and ran and the street kept getting longer and the street became a studded metal beltline that moved and moved against the way the son was running, and the son ran past a new man in the scrunched light pounding a drum kit and he ran past a man at a table eating a sandwich bigger than the earth and he ran past many other men who tried to ask him questions and all the men resembled the same man and the son felt the drumming banging in his ears and more dogs ran past him from the opposite direction and the dogs were dragging something and he could hear the dogs around in all directions coming and he could hear the sucking of a fan or vacuum from above, and he came to a street sign that looked familiar, but the next sign said the same thing, the streets all said the same thing, no matter how far the son went, and the flat long treadmilled concrete of the ground beneath him began to go soft and turn to mush, and the son was stepping high and hard like a bandleader and the son was trying to say a word and the son could hear the man still drumming and now with the drumming there were guitars, a heaving bass that made the air bend, and the drums were louder, and the word, and the son's calves were hulking, and the muscles bloomed with tumor, and the dogs were out there somewhere ripping clean and the son cried out and could not hear it and his skin was sledding off him in long coils, and liquid sluiced in rivers from his eyelids and out through metal straws now stitched into his head, kinked in long loops with bulbs and boilers and then back down into his mouth into his throat and the son gulped and drank his gushing wet and he found his tears refreshed him and he found his head sprayed open as a fountain— his head congealing, becoming lighter, blooming upward, bending in, he felt his new head mashed inside itself recoiling and the head began to take on new weight, and soon the head

was very heavy and the son could not control the sound, and the son lay down spread out against the vinyl floor—he felt it spread around him, one drawn and endless flat adhering and the son could not quite move and did not want to—and then the sky was bowing—and then the sky was just above.

IN THE SAND AROUND A HALLWAY

The son could not see right & yet he felt his body moving. He felt the air corral around him, days. He felt his feet ascend some stairs. A tugging on his arm hair. Field of moo. A beeswax blurb. **Hello.** He put his hand into it & was swimming. Something fell out of his mouth. He was above a lake then. He was floating. He could not make his eyes come open. He didn't want to.

The air was flaxen then—was rubber, then was wetted, then was cream. The air was nothing. There was all— some thick black crap crammed in around his head. The son began negotiation. He found that with his sharpest teeth—*more knives*—he could bite in and to and through the nothing air. The son bit & chewed & swallowed. He saw a crack of light. In the light there was some of somewhere. The son chewed & chewed & chewed & chewed & chewed & by each inch through which the son chewed he found no matter how much he could swallow,

his

mouth

was

al-

ways

full.

NOTHING YOU EVER, NOTHING NOTHING

The black creation that'd been seated on the neighbor's house's front lawn all this time had by now spread around the structure, further on. It had covered over the old doors and windows with new doors and windows, such as the one the son had come to stand in front of, sopping wet. The son did not see the swelling structure. The son did not see the street, nor his own house there beyond the pavement—*the same house they'd lived in all these years, they did not know they'd never moved.* The son couldn't see much for all the glaring—*even if he had seen, even if he wanted, his house would not be there.* The son felt sure that he'd arrived.

Yes.

Yes, in one of the windows in the house's face he saw the girl there smiling. The girl's soft head, shaped like his. He waved. He waited. He knocked and knocked and rang the bell. The girl was no longer in the window. The house was all around.

The son thought maybe there was something he had not done. Some invocation for invitation. He took out again the girl's directions. In fear unknowing, he'd stuffed them down his pants. He found now in his running, all his nowhere, the heave and screaming, drenched, the paper had adhered to the son's skin. Stuck to him, hugging, tingle. As the son pulled the paper off his body the paper ripped and became paste. It left small tattered patches near the son's navel. On the son's stomach the ink had transferred backward. The son could read the symbol words. The son spoke aloud each line, tasting language. In the list now the son found an instruction he hadn't read before, writ in new blue markings on his belly—a new tattoo.

The son did exactly as his skin said.

ANOTHER FUCKING BOX

Out in the street there, hours over, among the mist of night the father came upon a box. He could not remember the box he'd seen out on the neighbor's lawn all those days or weeks before. This box here was much like that box, of the same texture and shade, except bigger and giving off a stream of steam, sent out to mesh and branch upon the night.

The box here, in the middle of the highway—*how had he hit, at last, a highway? where were all the other cars?*—took up so much of the six lanes heading south—*six other lanes blockaded off beside them heading the opposite direction*—there remained no room on the blacktop for the father's car to fit around it. The box seemed to give away its own light, in flux of concert with the row of streetbulbs and skyspots overhead.

Under the loom of lamp the father slowed the car approaching, stopped before the box, got out. He left the engine on behind him, burning power.

Up close the box smelled like the son. The father had never had a particular stench he associated with the child's air, but here it was the first thing that he thought—like charcoal and like money, cake batter or a freshly painted wall. The father put his head against the surface, listened. Inside, he heard a motor, churned—the same sound as his own motor, there behind him, clearly repeated in the box. As well, the sense of something softer hovered, inches from his head there, ear to ear.

Hello, he said aloud and heard the words come out all from him, and heard it also in the box repeated back. *Hello.*

Oh, he said, realizing. *Oh.*

He peered up toward his car. The windshield had fogged over so thick he could see no longer in. Something hulked behind the shading. *Heads.* He felt his eyes move in his head to see the sky above him, flat clean black.

This box was warm. The father knocked. He heard the knock as well repeated, two sounds from one move.

My name is . . . the father said, then waited, to hear the voice inside the box fill the sentence in, but it did not. Instead, an itch dragging up along his inseam, a spark of choir. *My name is . . .*

The father threw up on the ground. In the vomit, there were errors—strings not vomit, but language, light. The bunched up bits were writing something, words at once sunk into the ground.

The father's hair was longer now. He could not feel it.

The father walked around the box. He brushed his hands along the surface, after something—ridges, locks, or doors. At the corner, between where the highway's edges held the box in at its side, there was a little aisle of space where he could sidle down along the box's left flank, pressed in. He could not see from here how long the box went on. It seemed to stretch forever down the way, as if the whole highway from this point and thereafter were seated with it, hosting. A light far beyond it gave it size.

The father hesitated at the box corner, not quite blinking, then he began along the box. His belly rubbed. His backbone. Inseams. Friction. The grain of the box, unlike the concrete median, was soft but firm—both wanting and somehow giving.

On the north side of the highway, there behind him, the father felt an audience, all watched. The median between them dragged against his back's tagged body fat. What if the box grew larger, all of a sudden? He would be crushed.

Inside his chest, he heard applause.

Inside the box, as he squeezed sideways, onward, inside the box, too, he heard the brush of flesh on box.

Father? the father asked it.

This time from inside the box came no reply.

SOFT!

Somewhere sometime along the box shape, the father found a divot in its face—a small nudged spot where the flat black surface interrupted and gave the father's body space to stand. Looking from the divot back along from where he'd come, the father could no longer see the box's end, where he'd left the car alive and running—and still there, the other way, the box continued on—the same dimension stretching both ways out there from this divot, shaped distinctly in his size.

Above, the sky was shuddering with light. Day soon again already, the father thought, and felt the box sway, the ground beneath him skinny, pale.

The father turned to face toward the box. Black and flat, twice as high as he was, hard to tell when there was no light where box ended and sky began. There in the grain of it, some language. The father leaned his head close up to read. Instead the words were little pictures—

the father standing in the house, the father coughing, the father holding a hammer toward a door. In each picture, the father appeared so much clearer, tighter. The father tried to turn away. As he did, inside each image, the other fathers turned first, and then he himself could not. He closed his eyes.

Overhead the light was gone again, hid behind lids. A flesh or floor or wall behind the father moved around him, sealed him in—the box around him eating the air up—the same blank sort of air that filled his house's vents—washing in around his knees.

AIR

Among the black space of the box, now turning softer, now gone cushy, streaming, the father, aging, wormed. He could not tell at all where he was going. Every inch matched every inch.

Into the shape of box surrounding, the father walked into the box.

Every so often he would open up his eyes again slowly, unreleasing, buttons pressing in reverse. Walls around him. Stalls around him. Houses. All mass. Massed. Opening each instant. On in. On.

If there is one hole in any home there must be many, he heard himself shout somewhere inside him.

Outside his skin he heard the night.

SLEEPOVER

Inside the girl's house, the house seemed endless. The ceiling went too high. The walls were made of stone and cracked in patterns that pleased the eye. There were large pictures of women and of men—some the son could recognize. Or had seen once. Or he might have. Just now. The son felt a bubble in his foot birth. He felt the bubble bobble up along his belly and past his lungs before it burst. He called these *thoughts*.

The house had not seemed so large from the outside, or so gorgeous. The girl's parents must be rich, the son thought. Which was weird because at school the girl always wore such ratty clothes—weird humpy bags of browbeaten cotton from long-dead decades' smothered styles.

The girl's house was made of wire, wicker, marble, slick, and sand. It had no smell. The girl's house's walls were often mirrors. There was everywhere to walk.

The son spent several hours staring into the portrait over one mantel, a gleaming field of white on white.

The son turned around then. He turned and turned. Tied to the wall where he'd come in, the son realized a piece of string he hadn't seen there prior. The string looped around his middle like a belt. The son grasped the string and felt it simmer, half-electric. He slid his fingers, making static, zinging. Cold . . .

PATH

The son followed the
long string down a
hallway without a
ceiling and without
doors.

The walls along the hall were wet
and mirrored and left grease on
the son's hands, slipped in slats
of gold goo underneath him,

trying to stick him in one place.

There was a music playing some-

where, by a band that did not

actually exist.

blank music washed on and on and all through the house like blood bombs dropping, like skin

peeling off of trees in sheets, women becoming horses becoming dogs becoming light—a whole

slew of awful sounds that were not really sound exactly, but sound as an idea

The son could feel the sound

against his chest and where

his bones joined, meeting,

vibrating his canine teeth.

The son could sort of see.

The son

went up

a

stairwell

and

down a

stairwell,

the string

now

burning

in his

hand—

the string

singing

along

and on

and on

into the

house.

For long stretches rooms would repeat—the walls and width
identical from end to end. White light in wash, from
overhead: projectors. Locks without true doors. Doors
without true locks or knobs or seams.

A small eye in some pink wood watched him from underneath
the floor.

Hairy curtains. Gold glass in windows, looking out onto
long unblinking fields.

Black chandeliers with yard-long candles. Coffee tables
made of water.

Bees.

The son in one room sat down for some time
in a recliner, hearing his cells spin or moisten,
softly jostled, coming open or awake.

The son walked.

The son found a charcoal-colored elevator that would not go
up or down, but had one button for each year.

He found a room filled almost full with one white cube,
around which he could wriggle, pressed at both sides,
breathing in.

He found a voice behind a wall—the voice of his voice,
older, slowing—some time gone.

And another stairwell, and another, each one wet and rattled in its own way. Some of the conjunctions between stairwells would have huge holes in their floors—wide-open mouths down into further house or houses. Some landings would have four or fifteen stairwells leading from them, lending the son a choice of which to take, but for each the string would keep him clinging, rawing at his palm.

The rooms went on each way around him there forever, not a music.

The son walked and walked and walked and walked and walked and walked and walked and walked and walked and walked and walked and walked and walked and walked and walked and walked and walked.

HOME

Inside the house the father crawled on. His eyes were pouring liquid. Laughing. The hot air ached his eyes. He'd moved into the box until he recognized it, found sections of its breadth where he had been—where he had called home—when he had slept and ate and lived. He found himself again inside the house's vents, the streetlights and homelights there some- how connected, and the airspace, and the drift.

The father loved the smell baking the house now, like money being burned, like melting Christmas trees and wire, like . . . like . . .

Like days.

At the vent's first bend, the tunnel opened into a small pocket ridged with bubbles. There was a language in the metal, the pocket's domed walls cut with tiny engraved pictures of a

house. The father could not keep his eyes held clean enough to see into the windows. Behind him he could no longer see the bedroom's light. There was another kind of light inside the vent now, writhing. The light in liquid at his face. He felt hair growing out around him, from each one of his finite, numbered pores.

I am the oldest man who's ever lived, the father heard himself say, blank of thinking. I will still be here in this air here when everybody else is burned and gunked and gone.

The words became a new long vein inside his nose.

TUNNEL IN A TUNNEL IN A TUNNEL (IN AN EYE)

Along the vent again the tunnel opened further ahead into two. Soon the two made four, and four made eight, and so on. Each tunnel looked the same. At each the father chose by which one seemed to need him. Laughing harder. Gasping. *Blue balloons*. His scalp skin crisping hard around his head.

At sudden nodules in the network, the father found holes where he could see back into the house—the living room, the upstairs hallway—the walls there had been painted over black—in some rooms orange or yellow—screaming neon—though here the vents went so thin he could not fit through them, not even partly, just his arms. Some rooms had been filled with dirt or smoke or foaming. Some rooms were full of skin—other families, people, bodies—smushed. One hole into one very far room was the exact same size as his eye—through the hole he could see another small eye seeing. *His eye*. Light.

The tunnels unfurled on. The ceilings raised or floors grew lower. He could hunch, then he could stand. Soon the walls were so high and far apart he could not feel them at all. The floor beneath him made of sand. In his testicles a transient tingling, like someone crawling through an opening in him, through his guts and up his body, spreading out and up and on among his blood. There was more of him than ever.

WHAT

At another upstairs pucker the father looked out and saw the mother walking up and down the street. She had her head down looking for something. When she got to one end of the street she turned around. She walked back and forth and back and forth in slow procession, holding her left arm straight up over her head. In her hand, a wide gray steel umbrella. She was talking to herself. She had her hair done up expensive. She'd done her face. The father banged his fist against the window to try to tell her she looked the best she'd ever looked but the mother could not hear him or would not turn.

HELP YOURSELF

The girl's house's kitchen was enormous. There were cabinets lined from end to end. Many of the cabinets had been padlocked. From inside some there came a scraping. Pictures of the girl were hung all over—tacked up in tiny frames all up and down the walls and the ceiling and the floor. In some the girl looked very old—much older than the son remembered. In some the girl was an old woman, or a man? In some the girl had so much hair you could not see her in the picture.

The son's arms were rubbed with rugburn though he did not remember any rug. He couldn't remember ever leaving off the hallway. He couldn't think of when he'd closed his eyes.

The house contained no clocks.

On a massive gleaming stove there were several pots and pans and spoons and basins of

shifting size. The things smelled awful or they smelled good. Many pots had lids puffed up with overflowing. The kitchen counter was long and marble and very cold. The son touched it with his face.

On the tile over the stove in black marker or grease there was a note: I AM WASHING. I AM TIRED. I WILL FIND YOU WHEN I CAN. LOOK DOWN.

The son looked down. The son could not see anything about the floor. His legs were wobbling a little. He couldn't think of when he'd last eaten. Maybe several days. His stomach felt lined with ugly light. He turned to look at all the cabinets. He had no idea which one he should open.

In the first cabinet, the son found a long rack of enormous knives—beautiful, sharply made blades that showed his face back to his face. The knives were so huge—as tall as he was, with a book's width to the blade—he knew he couldn't take one, though he tried. The metal slithered hot against his body as he stuffed it down his shirt. It burned and fizzled at his chest flesh, becoming soldered. It hurt to rip it free. The aching son replaced the knife inside its holder and watched it look back at him and gleam.

Another cabinet was the size of a warehouse and was stocked with books from end to end. All the books were copies of the same book, rotting, stuffed so full there wasn't room to move.

In another cabinet there was a replica of the son's neighborhood complete with every window, every door. Unlike the others, the son could not pry the doors or windows on his own house open, nor could he see in through the glass. A tiny black gazebo sat in their house's backyard beside the pool. *A gazebo?* Even smaller bugs were clustered to it, working

at the roof. Some smoke rose from its gaps. The son touched the gazebo's tip, felt an incision. He sucked his thumb and closed his eyes. When he looked again, there were people, many of them, small and teeming, crowded in like ants. They moved on small magnetic tracks set in the ground around his house and the gazebo, wanting in. They had eyes that opened and real hair. Some were shouting, so soft, a shiver purr. They would not see the son above. In other houses the people moved from room to room, at their own mirrors, eating air. From certain windows came a song. The son felt dizzy, dangled upside down. He chose one of the many people and broke the bind off and brought its body closer to his face. The little head was staring, saying something. The son squeezed the tiny body tight inside his palm. Tighter. Tighter. A little bubble. Rumbling. **Pop**.

That small sound echoed in the son's ears: pop

                                          pop

                                                pop

                                                    pop

                                                    pop

POP!

The son looked up. Standing beside him there was a little man—scaly, pale, flat features—the man seemed very pleased. He had long arms and a longer mustache and he was dressed in a deep gray bellhop jumper with high-heeled boots, a black neck scarf, and, draped over his shoulders, a snakeskin jacket. He had the biggest teeth the son had ever seen. The teeth all looked like keys. The son was afraid at first that the man would bite. Instead the man got out a little chalkboard.

He wrote, traced in the old dust using his thumb: I HAVE NEVER BEEN OUT OF THE HOUSE.

He set the chalkboard down on the floor where, resting, the text changed: THIS HOUSE IS OUR HOUSE, YOURS AND MINE. The son did not see these newer words. He did not see the text change again.

The man laughed and clapped and splayed his hands—a blackjack dealer's flourish, followed by sneezing. He went over to another cabinet and reached inside and got a tray. He went to the stove and opened pots and spooned things out onto many little plates, still sneezing, not covering his holes. The man didn't say anything. He breathed hard. His spine looked ruined or crooked. When the tray was full—so much food, enough for several people—the man hoisted the tray onto his shoulders and pointed with his nose toward another cabinet door—a door shaped just like the son was—son-sized.

So, son? the small man intoned, key-teeth splaying, speaking with no tongue. He sneezed and winked. Shall we? Surely. Oh, by all means, apres vous, allons-y, 移动, proceed?

FILM

The son followed the

man into the cabinet,

down another

hallway, also shaped

like him—though this

one was much shorter

than the others and

there were little

nodules with TV

screens on them

playing films.

Some of the films the
son had seen, though
others were unlike
anything. Some of the
films looked like real
people doing real
things, walking,
eating, taking a
shower, laughing,
playing video games,
brushing teeth.

Some of the films
were quite obscene.

There were films of pigs and dogs being exploded—
films of women giving birth, and films of men with
women in the stage of birthing preparation (one of the
couples in the films looked most exactly like the father

and the mother but much younger, the son thought), and there were films of milk pouring from another familiar house's windows and its girders and its seams (*what house?* the son could not remember any house but this one he walked and walked and walked in now) milk that on contact with the air and sky around it turned to mildew and to cheese—cheese that would be someday soon sold and then eaten, sent back into other bodies, carried on. There were films of the son watching a film inside a film inside a house (*that same house again, what was this? what was the son inside there doing with his eyes?*), there were films of the son falling through a great and endless air, the rip of wind and endless light greasing his body, pulling the flesh back in his face, making him look older than he'd ever looked, even in the deepest hours of the night.

Each film looped forever unrepeating, roaring on and on inside its frame, watching the son pass with its blank eyes, negotiating light.

The son saw and did not see.

The son's eyes were changing colors.

The son turned his head to concentrate on following the back of the bobbing head of the little man with all the food. The man had a tic in his neck that made him spasm so hard the son thought the man was going to drop everything he carried, but just as the tics began to get most convulsive, *knobby knots, skin-held explosions*, the man's neck and back and spine at once shaking so hard he hardly seemed to touch the ground, his skin as heavy as the sky—inside the room then the films went off and there they both were, standing face-to-face inside a cube.

ROOM

This room—*made from calming*—was
stuffed full of flowers large as the son.

Some of the flowers formed a chair.

There was a gentle music
playing—tones that raised tiny bumps
under the son's hair.

The man motioned for the
son to sit down on the flower
and when he did the man sat
the tray down on the son's lap.

The tray was hot and heavy.
The son could hardly move. He
looked up to the man and as
their eyes met the man bowed
low down to the floor and as
the man's head touched the
floor the flowers rumpled and
the room went superdark.

PHOTOPERIOD

Inside the father's eyes, white.   A gold of many glows.

Around his head, a second head.   White-on-white-on-white.

.

a hunk of blank space, meat or ceiling,   *a white of darkness inside the son,*

mask or fervor, him or he, or she: they   *scourged and beeping, gone, going*

A gold of man glows, unfolding.

In stereo of stereos, so wide.

[Inside the second head, the father watched the space around his body shuffle, open, like a deck of decks of cards, into a house.]

[Inside the second head and house, a city spinning soft. A sea which in the open caused a closing, a collapse of all that ageless air same as it came.]

NIGHT

The mother grew, *filled up with nothing—cells in cells on cells*, a house.

CONSUME

In the light from off his forehead, the son still could see his hands. The dinner plate was larger than he'd imagined. Some of the dishes were labeled with square brass placards, many of which, by handwriting or in translation, the son could not at all read: pink meats and bruised fruit, slaws and sauces, all soft enough to eat without the teeth, and such reek.

Several other unlabeled items were the ones that tasted best. The son stuffed his cheeks to bursting. The son ate so much it seemed his teeth themselves were also chewing with other tiny sets of teeth—as if eighteen people lived there inside him—people in people—on and on. There was a drink that tasted like one thing until he wished it tasted like something else and then it did. The son ate everything on every plate. The more he ate the more he wanted.

This house was excellent, the son decided, spoke in a voice inside his eyelid. Whenever the girl showed up the son was going to ask if he could move in, or at least if his dad could get a job with the girl's dad.

Completing this thought, the son tried to go on and think the next thing and felt the same words thereon repeat: This house is excellent—*his screaming eyelid!*—Whenever the girl showed up he was going to ask if he could move in—*yes, please, now*—or at least if his dad could get a job with the girl's dad—*he needed.*

And the thought again. The thought again, rolled in warming foam inside his head. A tone. He could not shush it. It numbed his gums—the food gluing all inside him, singing, a blank recurring unto exhausted, fat-full sleep.

DATABASE

In the other house—the empty house—*where was the father?*—the mother went to Google search.

The mother had on a translucent negligee. The mother's face was wet.

The mother typed in: *man who fixed the mower.*

She saw a bunch of lawnmowers and some fires and a knife.

The mother typed in: *man in the house with so much sand.*

The search results contained texts about a man who'd built his house on sand, a man who made sand music, a movie based upon a book, thoughts on how to enjoy beaches, a man

who'd built his house on rock.

None of this was what the mother wanted, clearly.

The mother's elbows creased with chafe, indention. Her forearms were so thick.

The mother typed in: *he with such long fingers*.

The mother typed in: *he with teeth & gloves*.

The mother typed in: *him*.

The screen went white. She felt her belly bubble, throb. It made a beeping.

The mother looked at what she'd done.

ENTRANCE, PASSAGE, GALLERY

The father came out of the bedroom into the hallway and started down the stairs and then the stairs beneath him seemed to crimp in some way they had never before right there. The stairs seemed to cling against the father's feet and also were crumbling in. Even as he stepped down onto the surface of the landing in the foyer where the stairs had always ended—there facing the door into the outside—the father could not help but feel that the room he was in now at the bottom of the stairs was not the room that had always been at the bottom of the stairs, but another room of the same shape and make and color—slightly off. Something about the texture of the wall or the way the window glinted or the way the light came in from outside and graced the ground. Something about the words that had been said in that room before then not quite sitting.

The father put his foot in certain places the way he had so many other days and felt a different feeling than he'd felt then. His right eyelid again twitching—*inner houses*. The father

pinched and prodded at his skin. He punched himself hard in his chest, his gut, the sides. The vibration flexed through his body in other places: between his toes, against his scrotum (vessels), in his knees. His other eye sat waiting, clean.

The father moved from the landing to the next room, which on most days was the room where the family ate. They had just eaten there today, had they not? Were they not eating there right now? The dining table still sat smattered under the bright red tablecloth curtain, stained in all those places that would not wash out. It seemed slightly larger than it had once been, or the father smaller. The chandelier the father had hung himself there to replace the prior lamp—a lamp that refused to quit cutting in and out, the sockets zapping when he touched them—the chandelier was still intact—though this chandelier's crimped metal arms hung so much lower—the father could step right up and take a bite. He could fit the tiny frosted bulb glass into his mouth and huff it. With the glow washed up inside his cheeks the father looked upon the room.

THE FATHER, RECONSIDERED

The father could have done anything he wanted. He could have walked right out of the house. He could have gone to the airport and bought a ticket to Lithuania. He could have walked to the grocery store and climbed inside the freezer bin and pulled the bags of broccoli over his face. He could have become a male prostitute and fucked for cash in bathrooms with his head beating in rhythm on the toilet tank. He could use the cash to buy stocks that would skyrocket and make him very rich, rich enough to live somewhere alone for the rest of his life and not stare at boxes in an office and not speak to anyone again. Not ever. At any moment, any of these things, the father could have done them. The father did not do any of these things.

ANTECHAMBER, SECOND ANTECHAMBER, SHAFTS

The father left the room with the table and entered another room that the family did not have a name for. The father did not like the way he felt while standing in this room but he also felt that he did not want to ever leave it.

The father craned his head into the next room, which was a hallway, and the father looked and looked. The father closed his eyes. He thought he heard someone else enter the room he'd just come from. He felt light bending around his back.

The father looked again and closed again. He had to leave this room, he knew, but he did not want to touch the hallway carpet and he could not go back the way he came. The hallway carpet had a peculiar pattern.

The father held his breath and jumped across the air.

The father landed in another room. *There were tiny holes in this room that looked out onto exact geographic coordinates of space.* The father opened up his eyes.

The father had aged by eighteen months.

The father was at an age when eighteen months would not vastly change his outward physical appearance greatly, though some more of his hair had fallen out or molted white. His joints creaked in their gristle. His skin continued to sag. The father's teeth bent slightly inward and were corroded slightly in color and dimension. His vision degraded enough to make him ineligible to pilot a motor vehicle. His other insurance premiums increased by 18 percent. His intestines loosened and the tapeworms inside them multiplied

and slithered in their widths. The father's brain blew fat with wrinkle.

Around the father in the house the rooms were there. Through the years these rooms would fill with things and some of those things would stay and remain the same unless moved or acted on by outside forces and other things in the rooms would come and go— this is what science had let him know. For the majority of their existence the rooms would contain nothing, and the nothing would not change.

FILM OF A FILM

In the room the father could not see one
end of the room or the other. He could not
see his fingers or his hands.

The father's feet were on the floor, he felt
sure. He was breathing through his mouth.

A camera may have floated through the dark-
ness—*dark was all that held the house together.*

The father moved forward through the
room in one direction. He could not feel
his body go.

The father tried again.

Around the father the room went some-
where and in the room the father went into
it and the father was there and the father
moved.

He did not realize he was shouting. His
voice enclosed around his head. He shook
his head to get the sound out, and again
began shouting, turning red:

This is my house.

This is our house.

This is where I am.

MAP OF ASCENT

The father went

—through a room he recognized into a room he did not recognize, *each in exact image of the room where he'd been born*

—into a room hung with photographs of people the father felt sure he did not know, *he could no longer recognize his father, his father's father, his father's father's father, as well as several other men with his blood in them, and so on*

—into the room where the mother had figured she'd someday find time to do her sewing, making bed quilts out of old clothes, *instead the room had grown so thick with dust you could no longer see the walls*

—into the room that'd most sold the father on the house for no particular reason he could put a thumb on, *six walls slanted inward up to some center overhead, a leaving point, a sight*

—into a room that was all windows, the glass gurbled, spurting, off, through which window the father saw only color that was not like any color unto him before, *the compiled color of the lengths of skin he'd bruised upon himself and certain others over the fearful evenings of his life*

—into a room made of liquid in which the father could swim deep into one corner and could touch something there giving off air, a tiny rimless hole, and the father put his mouth against it and he breathed, *inhaled the smell of gasoline and cinder and gunpowder and new cars, and there were objects consecrated there around him in the liquid, held within a gel, he could not see*

—into a room of cold wet sand tunneled by worms, *worms that once had lived inside the son, and ate of all the food the son ate, making a blank space, and heard of all the sound he heard, and sang in all his singing, and wallowed in his light*

—into a room of babies held in long glass bubbles burping, screeching, needing feeding, waiting for their size, *each of which would one day make their own sons and daughters, and those their own sons and daughters, and theirs, and theirs, more and more blood*

—into a room lodged in the bulb glass of some light fixture in a woman's apartment in some city, where the father watched the woman remove her clothes and masturbate against a mirror and brush her teeth and wrap her head in string, *the father wanted this woman more than any one or thing he'd seen in his whole life, and did not realize how she looked exactly like the mother, named the same*

—into a room the father had already been in before this evening but not in the same light, not like this, *to be honest all of these rooms had the same shape and grain and color, each measured 5.24 m × 10.48 m × 5.86 m*

—into a room where the father was hardly dust and the father could not feel his arms, *his hair around him in a coarse gown, as one day he would be buried under sand*

—into a curtain of endless blank where there was laughing, *every person, all at once, one thick and endless sound so loud it went beyond human hearing and beyond that again, killing all ears, breaking all windows in all buildings, shattering all light, and then replacing all of what it had damaged with new versions of itself, so deftly done we'd never know*

—into another room made of something other, *the description of this room has been withheld by request*

—through a room he recognized into a room he did not recognize, *each in exact image of the room where he would die*

APEX

In this last room the father touched the wall and slid against it and the father was on the floor there looking up—through the ceiling the father could see some clouds convening, or were they clouds or something else. Something unraveled, something blackened, threaded through and through and through, and in this last room, from another, in a far part of the house, someone was shouting something awful in the soundshape of the father's other name, and the father turned toward the name, his insides lifting, and the ceiling flexed with all his work and in the center of the ceiling a new hole opened and through the new hole came an eye, which there, then, saw.

LAWN

Outside the house the grass around the house—the dead and endless grass the mother had mowed and mowed in begging to keep down—the grass with no roots left to mention, their butt ends frayed into a mush—roots that once had spread embedded underneath the other nearby houses in a network, a scumming labyrinth, a kind of whip—by now this dead and pure white groan-grass had grown up a few feet high. It grew to just below the house's windows and grew up around the doors and at the outsides of the walls. It grew up beneath the house beneath the father and the father could feel it tickle, screaming, other language, through his chest.

HI HEY THERE HELLO

The son felt a warmth flood through his skin. Gumming. Groggy. Mental sunshit. Metal wash. He could not get his eyelids open. He felt pressure running in one ear. His corneas felt fat—so big behind his eyelids that they groped and grapped and stuck. The son rolled and moaned for someone. So many colors washed his mind—the color of every room he'd ever been in, one after another, roto-flashed, became white. To match the color, *somewhere counting*, the son heard a snake of language at his ear—every word he'd ever said replayed together, compressed into one brief, marbled gob. The words were coming slightly out of the son's mouth. He was saying things he'd said before. He could hear himself but nothing else. He didn't want to say it. The son's nostrils allowed something in then something broke off and then the son's head throbbed through sinking and he could see.

The girl was standing above him. Her arms were flexed with muscle through the gloves. Their heads were held together, inches. The girl was breathing in his breathing and he was breath-

ing in the girl's. Up close, the son could see the girl was wearing the locket he'd tried for years and years to throw out, its clasp unclicked. The son looked to see the tiny picture there inscribed: an image of him looking at him, covered in black hair, a ring of bees surrounding the tight perimeter of his two whiteless, gleaming pupils, in each of the eyes another son reflected, and in those eyes, and in those. As far back into the aisle of eyes as he could see the son saw him there, seeing. Then the eyes blinked, *all at the same time, with the son's.*

They were in another room. There was a sofa, TV, rug, and chairs. Too many chairs. The walls were painted yellow. The room was small and common as any other room ever elsewhere, *any room*. Up close, the girl's face looked like his. Her eyes were massive—cracked, bejeweling. The girl stepped back. The girl had boy's clothes on—the same clothes the son had worn into the house. They clung tight on the girl's soft body, showing weird tones and ridges in her skin. The son looked and saw now that he was dressed in a white gown, made of lace and ribbon with his full name stitched across the front. The name was written inverted so that he could read it plain by looking down. The gown clung at his throat.

I made that for you, the girl said, sighing. Or had it made. Regardless. Do you like?

The girl was holding a little plastic egg. The egg was made of tiny pieces that folded in or up and out, by which the egg could be modified or disassembled. The girl rummaged through the egg's configurations absentminded as she watched the son from where she stood against the wall. The egg became a prism, became a thought, became a gun. The girl held it up to show him, near her temple. The egg made little clicking sounds.

The son opened up his mouth. The son was burping bubbles. He felt something crawl inside his throat. He felt his lips go smile and forehead nodding. The son sat up a little. His cheeks were raw. He felt heavy, full of something.

The girl was watching him intently. Are you hungry? Her skin rasped, making noise. The skin rashy, pockmarked, curdling.

The son felt his lips unlock.

The butler fed me, he said, in spouting old voice, then again he could not speak.

What butler? the girl said. What butler?

The man in the kitchen, the son said bending, another guttural gush. A little gray man. Sneezing.

The girl just showed her teeth and winked her eyes.

A VERY SPECIFIC WALL

The girl moved to stand against the wall. She turned and looked at where she was against the wall and moved a little to one side. They were both quiet for some time. The house was quiet. The same air in and around the house.

The girl wasn't holding the egg anymore, at least not where the son could still see it. The girl was chewing on her lip, and chewing hard. She had a new bulge to her belly. In his own mouth the son swallowed and felt something go down. The son looked across the room. The girl was there. She had something written on her face. She saw the son watching. She pulled out a small white stepladder and climbed up on it and did a dance. Her belly from this angle appeared caving. She grinned and hulked it in and out and out and in.

One of the room's white walls began to shake.

So what do you want to do now? the girl said, bubbling above the sound.

PORTAL

The father opened up his eyes. What he'd made in the wall where he'd located the un-
wanted indentation was like a puckering, a way out or way in. The father punched the
center of the shape with his fist and listened as it fell into the hole. Then the wall was
open. The father put his head inside and peered around.

Inside, the space was roughly large enough for an average-sized adult. There wasn't
enough light to see much else. The father pulled his head back out and took the hammer
and began to jack at the opening with the butt-end, ripping away chunks of sheetrock in
showers. The head of the hammer, cold. The hole began to widen, its pucker yawned. The
father dropped the hammer and pulled at the flaky edges instead with his whole hands,
dust falling on the carpet, on his shoes and in his hair. He flung the pieces behind him,
yanking and sweating, ticked up in some kind of bizarre joy. He could feel the particles in
his nostrils, down his throat—bits of the house.

On the stubborn pieces, hung with nails, he pulled harder, at one point ripping a long cut down his forearm. His bright blood dripped in neon light. The color wept into the fiber, and the wood beneath, another layer. The father didn't stop. His heart throbbed now more than he could last remember. He felt good. His head was light.

He picked the hammer up again and set it down again. The room spun around the father as if on an axis, some translucent wheel. And the music. He heard music somewhere— inside him—a song he knew he knew he knew. So much music, the father thought. He touched the wall.

The father laughed.

QUEEN

On the floor above the father, the mother had risen up. The mother knew she needed some-
thing but could not think of what or how to name it, how to put her hands in a way that
would bring that something closer or quell the ache. The mother did not realize she was
naked. The parents' bed had moved. The parents' bed sat against the wall opposite from
where it'd been last. Their sheets were wet and upside-down. The designs on the sheets—
same as those in the son's room, and the guest room, and elsewhere in the house—showed
backward through the fabric, becoming something.

The mother moved beyond the bed. She went into the bathroom where the sink and bath-
tub overflowed. The floor was slick with wet from both. The water had not touched the
bedroom carpet. The mother stepped into the water. She did not see anyone in the room.
She did not see the father or the son or the other father. The mother walked back out into
the hall.

The mother went down the hall to the door to the son's bedroom and put her hand against the door. She beat the shape and knocked and called his name out. Name! Name! she said, croaking. Son! Son! She shook. The door would not come open. Her wet feet had not left a trail behind her on the carpet.

The mother put the lock against her eye. Through the lock she could see nothing. She took her eye away. She replaced the place where her eye had been with her mouth and blew through the keyhole into the door. *The mother had learned this trick.* Her breath was made of air and water, laced with house dust. The mother touched the knob again. The door came open. Inside the son's room as well the bed had moved from one wall to another—through the wall the parents' and the son's beds had come to kiss. The wall seemed to bow slightly between them. There was a sound but not a sound.

On the floor, bunched on the carpet, the mother saw a box. The box was neat and had black coating. The box did not have seams. The mother moved. The windows rattled. Her cell phone rang. She could not hear it. She could not hear. Her neck muscles pinched, contracting. Her right thigh began to spasm. The mother stood above the box. She nudged it with her foot. The box didn't move much. In the grass below the window something thrashed or rattled. The mother squatted on her popping haunches. Her nails and hair were getting longer. The box rotated. Her eyes burst vessels. There was a sound but not a sound. Around the house the trees were bending. The mother took the box and made it shake.

THE HOUSE WAS GETTING WAVY

What was that? the son said, slurring. What is it?

He tried to hide behind his hands. His mouth filled with a thin, translucent goo.

The girl kept looking at him.

The son could not blink.

COPY HOUSE

Just past the short, brushed shaft he had uncovered behind the wall there, the father found another house. An exact copy of their own house—a copy kitchen, den and bedrooms, and so on. The replica connected in mirror to the air where during the day they ate and night they slept. The copy house had the same furniture and junk as the other—same pictures, carpet patterns, rub marks, dishes in the sink—though here their personal adornments, family items had turned a smoke-licked shade of black. Black bulbs, black quilts, black clothing—black food cartons, utensils, mail. Only the doors, floors, and walls—the body of the house itself—remained the same as in the other, if made paler by their darker contents in relief.

As well there were no windows in the walls where to look out onto a light. In locations where in the first house there had been a glass pane, instead the house appeared fully sealed. There were no keyholes in the doors or ways to peep through. No vents or holes

beyond the way the father had ripped in. The black clocks all read a certain number. Each black bowl or black glass left out had been turned over upside down, holding its air.

The table in the dining room was shorter, stacked with clean plates, finger bowls. A square black cake—oblong, like an office building. The father touched the icing. Smoke rose in sigh, and stunk. The father tried to wipe the icing off. A tingling. It clung hot to his skin—to his fingers and his shirtsleeve and the tablecloth and air. He rubbed it on the wall there, his fingerprints repeated, smudged.

The father tried to call out into the house around him but his air would not come out—the quick words caught inside him, wobbling. His breath burned in his holes.

In the hall, along the long wall, someone had made a mural of, the father surmised, the sun being crushed into the moon? It was hard to say what was there exactly, but something bright and muddy. Words were written in the pigment's ridges that the father could not read, or else the words were numbers, small directions. Some seemed to shift when he turned from them. The small door that had before opened into the hair closet was no longer there. The father's nose began to bleed.

The guest bedroom door was locked. Behind the door, some muted choral moan: low tuba, a beaten box, a gong. Blood from his ears now, too, a little. Throbbing in his eyes.

In the den the books had been turned to face their spines toward the wall. The pressed-together pages packed in grinning, silent with their billion flattened teeth. The father took down a skinny volume, flipped it open, found the pages fudged with see-through gel, lined like a cell inside a hive.

He passed the wall again where the mural had been just before, and in its place a mirror hung. The father was wearing dark pants and a dark shirt, he realized, though he'd come in wearing blue. He had the black cake icing on his face and arms and in his hair and on his teeth. Blood from each hole, a set of greasy spigots, rolling. He was wearing gloves and smoking a cigar. Each inhale, in the mirror, twinned. Each blinking, posed. He was so old.

The hole the father had hacked in through watched him walk back along the carpet to the front room where the front door also had been sealed. No drip of blood or mud or must on any inch of any.

Here the stairwell to the second floor, the father found, went down instead of up.

REMEMBEREMBERER

When the son looked again they were in another room. He'd been laid prostrate on a long deep red sofa with an awning that hid the ceiling from his head. The room held several mirrors. The girl stood behind him, behind the sofa. The girl combed the son's hair. The hair had so many knots and nits slipped in it. The son felt okay. The combing stunk.

Why weren't you at school last week? the girl said.

The son felt a spasm in his eye. I was at school, he said. I thought you weren't.

The girl hummed a little song.

Whenever the girl's knuckle brushed the son's scalp, he felt it burn.

What butler? the girl repeated. She laughed out through her nostrils. She tugged hard on the son's hair. In his cleaned locks, she threaded rings, translucent to the light.

The room they'd come to now was long and thin and had one enormous window, though from where they were sitting the son could not see out. The light changed direction and intensity every several seconds, revealing different parts of the long room. In one section the light revealed a corridor down which the son could hear many other people singing, the same song as the girl. In another section the light revealed a fountain and a man standing at it with his back toward them, completely still.

In completely different light entirely the son saw on the wall behind the girl several long black bags hanging—bags like the one he'd found inside the box. These bags had shapes inside them that stretched their fabric. Some bags were bulgy, flush with weight, while other bags seemed to handle almost nothing. Some of the bags were wet in places. Each one had a tag sewn onto the zipper, filled in another kind of script—names and numbers, illegible descriptions of their contents, where they'd come from, how they'd been. There was at least one bag for every picture the son had seen inside the box, including his—his long black bag hung there on the wall there, open—and many more beyond. Bags and bags unending. It was hard to look at any of them very long. There was no smell inside the room.

The son realized, in the seeing, how he did not actually remember the bag from his own house or the box or his father and mother or his house itself or the house they'd lived in before that one or how he'd come into the house here or how he'd met the girl—these bags had only been in this room here, ever—he wasn't sure how he knew he realized this. The son's forehead wormed with flexing meat. He laughed and laughed. He loved the bags. He loved *his* bag, the skin of its inseam. He loved this house and all the people and the walls that held them in. The son loved the couple who'd come to see and touch the walls inside

the other house, their replication, *the couple carrying his want.* The son loved the slick of sound inside him never ending and loved how he could no longer feel his mouth, his hair pulled down so hard around his skull he needed nothing more than nothing, than the hour of his skin, cells given from the width of many others, in thunder, money, wishing, laughter, need, and mud. He would love this house forever. His house. This girl. He. Hers. Him. The rivers of the air inside his blood in prisms. Evenings.

The son shook his head, looked up by looking down.

His mouth filled up again with nothing—he swallowed hard.

I like to remember things my own way, like anybody, he said, in a second voice, with words that were not words.

DRINK

The girl laughed louder than the son had. She laughed so hard her eyes shook and she spanked the back of the son's head and tugged his hair harder than hard and laughed again so loud the air was older and made the son slap her hand with his. She fell back against the wall of bags, disturbing several, *the sound of cymbals and of paste*. She writhed across the floor. Her body seemed to dance, contorted. Her eyes rolled back in her head. Her neck was bending. Her neck seemed putty. The walls went wrinkled. The son started to stand up. Instead the girl stood up and caught her breath and waved for him to stay. She crossed the room and opened a panel in the ceiling with her long arms—*the son had not noticed how long her arms were*—and came back out with a can—a fist-sized chrome can with no label but engraved shit the son could not read. She set the can down on a tray. She brought the tray over to the son and stuck a long curled straw through the can top and helped the straw into the son's mouth. The straw was made of something neither plastic, metal, wood, nor bone. It seemed to fit his teeth.

Drink, the girl said. It is delicious.

The son could not disagree—though the substance was not liquid—nothing there but air at all.

He drank.

the house there all around him, ashing

all through the roof and walls, unwound

in light, his name shaking out its color

shaking out its hours, numbers, nouns

THAT IS SOME THICK STUFF

The girl watched the son drink, then took the tray away and went back in place again to comb. She yanked the son's hair back so hard on his head his scalp strained red, exposed. The son's scalp had tattoos all through it. The tattoos were of text fine-printed, writ by hand. The hair was held back by a series of small pins that pulled the hair's roots so tightly they seemed ready to rip out any minute. In the mirror across the room the son could see himself aligned. He could see his room a little, his other room, in that old house. He felt the house inside him, in the mirror, its glass now leaning right against his face. This particular mirror, the son noticed, close up—*among the many rooms refracted*—this mirror was the same mirror as the one he'd slept with every night. This particular mirror was caving inward there against him, curving, becoming jelly, burble, white. In the mirror now, the son gleamed, of no expression.

RORRIM

The girl saw the son was looking. She let the son's hair fall free and took the son's chin. She seemed to be saying something. The heat was foaming. The son could not shake it off. He could not not. The house's color bloomed. He felt something move inside him, metastasizing, filling his form with its form: *smoke through smoke, room through room*. The son reached back and touched the girl's arm. Her skin was smiling.

So what do you want to do *now*? the girl said.

NOT A WORD OR SHAPE OR NAME

The other floor's long hall of bedroom doors all stood open, stunk and stung the father's

eyes. The wet revolved inside his head and made him hungry, stuck with an itching, in

the light. He held his hands upon the air there, flush with hot flashes—a drum kit in his

lungs—his feet swollen beneath him, doorbells. The other house alive.

The floors down here were mirrors. The father watched himself walking from below.

Each step made him thicker, narrowing the walls.

In spasmed gulps, the way his childhood cat had—*the cross-eyed, many-named creature*

who one night had crawled into a mudhole in the woods behind his parents' house and not come

out—its name still somewhere in him, its absent sound—the father coughed something up

into his hands: an origami box folded out of wet, smeary flash paper—with it at last out

of his chest he could see head-on again—he could think of things he'd seen once: ash

rising from fires, balls thrown, nipples tugged, bundles of cash. The father unfolded the origami, hearing it crinkle, as did each day the fat filling his head. WHO IS IN THERE, someone had written. The father ripped the note into many tiny pieces and swallowed it again.

In the house the hall held still. Somewhere above him a pucker shrunk a little, released a smudge of air. Black and magnets. Runny.

The father walked along the hall. He stopped outside the copy master bedroom. He turned to face the light. In the room he saw his body sleeping, several of him. The furniture had been removed. The bodies of him piled into the small space stacking, puddled up with limbs. Some were missing hair or digits. They were cuddling, chewing, talking in their sleep. Laughing, scratching, humping, what have you. The more he looked the more there were, though sometimes, between blinking, there was just him, *well, he and the him inside him*, and the meat around his seeing, and his arms. The father closed his eyes and heard them breathing, heard his many hungry stomachs snarl.

With his hands within the forced dark, the father closed the door.

The father felt his way along the hallway further, palms along the walls. In the grain, the house had written out a list of names, a man's phone number, a tablature, a hymn's words, a prayer, a map, a day—none of which the father understood as language, *and yet it settled in him still*.

The father felt along the hall with all his fingers till he felt another door. This door would be the son's door, the father said, and heard his body say. The door into she and I and his

320

and hers and ours and ours and our son's room. This door as well was open, *another mouth inside the copy house*—or was he back inside his own house now? The father could not tell.

His chest was throbbing.

The father moved into the room. He moved onto the air with skin around him, feeling forward, unwilling yet to open back his eyes.

INTERVIEW

The girl moved in a little closer. She had her hands behind her back.

The girl turned into the mirror—turned to look at **someone else**.

The girl began to speak, in several voices, asking someone:

Q: WHAT DID THE SON WANT TO DO?

Q: WHAT DID THE SON WANT TO WANT TO DO?

Q: WHAT DID THE GIRL WANT FOR THE SON?

Q: WHAT COULD THE GIRL HAVE DONE TO MAKE THE SON WANT SOMETHING ELSE?

Q: HOW MUCH HAD THE SON EATEN? HOW MUCH HAIR COULD FIT INSIDE HIS CHEST?

Q: HOW MUCH COULD FIT INSIDE THE GIRL'S HOUSE? THE SON'S HOUSE? THE COPY VERSION(S)? WHY?

Q: WHAT WAS THE GIRL'S HOME MADE OF? AND THE SON'S SKIN? AND THE GIRL?

Q: WHAT FIT IN THE SPACE BETWEEN THE HOUSES?

Q: WHO ELSE WAS COMING BY?

The girl was turning. The girl glowed. The son glowed.

Q: DO YOU KNOW NOW?

Q: DO YOU?

Do you?

THE WANTING BOX

In the image of the room where nights the son would be, the father felt his body press against another hold. He opened his eyes, saw nothing but it—a black box large as the whole room. It gave off a silent steam or smoke, as had the last box he remembered, which upon remembering in that instant he ceased to remember furthermore.

The door the father had come into the room through was no longer there behind him, nor was there much of any space left for him to stand between the box and wall. He had to suck his gut in, skin into skin there, held not breathing, and still there was hardly room for him to move—as if he were underneath the box at the same time as above it, and beside it—nothing but the box—no room at all.

Inside the box, a bumping. Something smothered. Rub of skin of fists. The father pressed his head against the surface, wanting. He listened harder, leaning in. The more he leaned,

the more he had to—his spine took kindly to the curve—then, there he was leaning with all of him against the image, its surface adhered to his shoulder and his cheek.

The round meat of the father's left ring finger puffed up. *More rings*.

Father, the father tried to say back, and out came all the other names.

He tried to speak again and still could not, the words instead reflected in his head, spurting as would a heavy wet through his cerebrum and down into his chest and ass and legs, and no repeat.

The father's face against the box, both of them aging, one changing shape inside, one not—his body flush against the box's, gripped.

The no light coming through no windows to the no room to the need.

In all his want, and all the surface, the father's head became pressed upon so hard against the box he could not see—or could not tell what he was seeing, in such color—the bend of wall on wall, the blank—gone windows lit with light of leaving, sucked from the house into the sky. The box pulled on his backbone, barfing through his body in reverse—warm milk, spit, rainwater, stomach acid, fresh blood—his body sticking to the seam, wherever. In his head he heard a hundred guns—a fall, a swallow, sinking—*black cells*—then, there he was above him, and beside—then, there he was below him, and between him, and overhead, within—he could see himself from every angle—he could see himself inside the box.

INSIDE

The box

inside was

small at

every

angle—so

small the

father had

no room to

move his

arms or

legs or

head.

The inner
surface of
the box,
unlike its
outside,
held a ripe
transparent
pale—so
pale there
appeared
not to be a
surface
there at all,
unwinding
—and yet
against the
father's
flesh it
made a
pressure
and
against the
father's
flesh it
burned.

To the left
and just
above the
father's
vision in
the box
there was a
hole—a
single tiny
source of
seeing
allowing
light onto
the pupil
of his right
eye.

Through the
hole, the
father saw a
grayish
chamber.
Inside the
chamber hung

                                              another eye,
                                                 like the
                                              father's eye
                                              but larger,
                                            with lid and
                                               vein and
                                                cornea
                                              removed.

In the light inside the eye the father saw another light—*it had a name*—a name he could
not hear or say or see inside him, though it was watching—seeing—seen. The father
                     could not think beyond the what.

The eye had many sides. Each time the father blinked inside his own sight within the other's—*quick black*—when he looked again the eye would seize. The eye would spin among its sides and scrunch like aged skin, then come to settle centered on another side. Each new side held a new pupil to look into, and it looking back as well, again.

Through each pupil, paused before him, the father felt

a force of light thread through his head—

light of photographs without color—

light of music without sound—

light of books without pages—

light of paintings without paint—

light of dance without limb—

light of speech without lung—

light of buildings without walls—

In deleted air the father saw the ageless light of those the light itself had made destroyed—one for each side of the eye here in the box here in the copy house around the father, stunned with the light of skin in skin deleted young—like those in the pictures the father's son had been sent, the son among them—bodies organed with creation of an hour never named—deleted light held inside daughters, inside sons.

The light came in all through the father, frying.

In the light the father saw:

, [44]

, [45]

[46]

&

. [47]

The father saw:

,48

,49

,50

,51

,52

,53

,54

,55

,56

,57

,58

,59

,60

---

48 *the curtains in the living rooms changing their color and then back again, just off—*

49 *a ring of blood welled in the pages of the center of every instance of a certain book—*

50 *the mattresses filling up with hair or fire—the mirrors blanching briefly clear—*

51 *one white hair grown out on all dogs surrounding—*

52 *from all the keyholes in the house, an O-ing moan—*

53 *the pianos' least played key becoming detuned—a spore inside the bass guitars—*

54 *some location in one wide ocean turning harder among the froth—a softest plot—*

55 an era without era; blank and silent light and sound

56 a book that erupts water—

57 a tone that shifts the lid of sky—

58 a film of all film looped forever underneath the lip of ground—

59 a room of rooms—

60 *a sentence written in the center of the chalk—*

61 *backward laughter in the orange juice, frothing gently—drowned—*

62 *translucent mold inside the bread loaves—*

63 *cogs at the center of the sun—*

64 *a sticky syllable pronounced in our cerebrums, eating—*

65 *an alphabet dissolved—*

66 *the earth for one half second rendered flat and upside down—*

67 the father upside down and laughing, also—the son in 3 rooms at 1 instant—

68 the mother again gushing, pregnant—the mother full of passing time—

69 *more light—*

70 *houses kissed each with new rooms, days and hours—*

71 *neighborhoods each with new inches, walls—*

72 *cities groaned to grow around a pucker, scrying—*

73 *opened;*

       ,74

     75

    &

    .76

There were many other sides upon and in between each side that the father could not sense seeing, even deleted, but which came into him still.

When the light of each of all the sides was gone again in spinning, the light remained there still—it hung in gristle, caked in bones and teeth, in the ceiling of the nothing far above—in distance and in hours, doorways—reflecting air back at the earth—in all the dirt, and all the wonder—*days in hours—years in days*.

---

74 father, mother, infant—worn—

75 *another want comprised of nowhere—*

76 *another instant for the night*]

Inside the box inside his seeing, the father aged. Old sores on his body healed shut. New unseen sores began. His blood made bleeding, wanting. The father felt no tone.

Each time the eye shuddered in rotation a place inside the father's head would make a click—a long hot drop all through his body—*light beyond light*—and then, from nowhere, his eyes could see again. He went on in this condition, a finite binary upon his body suffered in repeat:

(a)   The spinning spheroid's next side.

(b)   The burst of light of light.

With each instance, the father screamed. He screamed so hard all through him and with every inch he felt his body, in that instant, become zilch. He could feel, in the periods in which he did the watching, such white-hot power-terror funneled through his blood and air and flesh that it was as if he never had existed, underneath such screaming, such massive, hobbling hurting, grief. He knew, upon each instance, that when it had passed it would be gone from him again—and yet would not be gone at all. Among all air. Upon the body. The gift ungiven in no glow.

As each click came, compiling, the father felt no terror and no rake—not even any itch for where the light came crushed against him—and in the end the father was still there—the father soft and strung inside the box inside the house inside the street inside the light inside the air that held the house among the void. The father's body eating both himself and nothing, son and father, light and no light, silence, sound.

And now this moment never happened

and this went on for quite some time

ANSWER

All the son could see, where he was, was milk and mirrors, knives.

The room was very gone. Beginning. The son turned inside him, on.

Then the son could see a color, then another color. Then a hole.

BOX OF BOXES

In the house again, beside the box, the father felt him, in his body, open up his age-less mouth—a mouth of skin and text and warm rain—and though still now in the room there with the box still words would not come out, and there from his father body came another shape instead, a glowing, flowing fountain through his center—a small ream of creamy water which, against his teeth and tongue, became another box,

a blackened nodule

in his mouth hole,

small as a bird's

egg, or a bulb:

And in the room there the father could see absolutely nothing but the sides and faces of the ejection, the new shape, each side there in the house there pouring brightly, and there against his skin the box began to spin,

giving off

an awfullllllllllllllllllll

stutterreddddd

soundddddddd

With each instance of the sound, the box blew even more light, glowed as if its heat would bend it in

and from the seam of what the box was it made an-

other, spitting more boxes from its shrieking o o o o o

another box there: O

and another: O

boxes falling out of boxes, boxes of boxes, boxes, glow on glow on glow—
the mother somewhere underneath it—as in spiral, as in stun—boxes spit-
ting up more boxes to make more boxes, blackened gifts

and as each box hit the air inside the house the house
would shake and ripple, there and there, and there—
shook like singing through blown speakers

rippled like clear light peeled off of some uncertain

sky

as each box fell, sent in its order, to shriek and shake upon the ground, the room quickly became filled in with the boxes—the more there were the quicker made—each box giving its own and from therein more and more, each of a light and sent in writhing, still unopened, mega-rubbed—

until box by box

by box   by box

the room was so bright

and the father, any of him,   *at the windows*

could not breathe

or sink or   say or

see

WHERE AM I WHERE HAVE I BEEN WHERE ARE YOU

& now the house was full of boxes   *houses*

& now the air around the house was full as well, swarmed & gathered at its walls & ceilings,
a silent sound   *a hall*

& now in the sky above the house of boxes light was rising
                                        & resizing

& now the father, son & mother at once in time together breathed—& in the same way they
had grew out of some center
                                        to the center they returned

Her neck was sore. She had an awful
twitch. Above the mother's head there
was a window.

Through the window you could see
into the backyard, where the light
was gushed and bronzing. The yard
had grown. The light was null. The
swimming pool had overflowed.
Black algae water sloshed the grass
and tore the sod up. The yard could
moan a little.

The copy father and the copy
mother, in the deep parts, floated up
and down and up.

FOUR

INTERVIEWER: *Do you think there will be a Poltergeist III?*

HEATHER O'ROURKE: *There should be because the beast is not dead.*

REMOVAL

Men came for the father in the morning. They arrived in inky shockgear—stained black jumpsuits with enormous kneepads for kneeling and fattened multicolor frays around their shoulders to make aiming at their heads much more confusing and long bright orange gloves that hid their skin while domed metal visors hid their eyes. There were seven men, but just one language. They also moved as one and ate one meal a day and slept in the same bed and knew the same woman with whom they'd made the same child. They worked for the same firm as the father. They were the future.

The father stood there in the kitchen. The father would not blink. He watched the walls that brought the room together, tracing the outlines with his eyes. He was waiting to see something. He was waiting for something to see. He'd wedged himself into a portion of the room where he felt he could see and monitor every inch. Still, when the father turned his head just slightly one way or another, he felt something loom on the perimeter. He could

not keep a straight face. Either he was laughing or he had his mouth scrunched to try to keep the laughter in. His stomach muscles burned. He hadn't eaten. Someone was knocking on the door.

The father continued to watch the room. The father did not want to leave the room and break his concentration. He knew things about the house. He had long words written on his arms in marker, maybe. His lips and neck were wet with running ink. In the photographs it would appear the father had just written his name over and over and then begun to sweat them off, but actually he'd been licking. He did not know about the licking. His tongue was filthy. His blood was unwell.

The father did not flinch as the door became kicked open. He did not struggle as the men swarmed in around. They restrained his legs and arms in plastic ticker. They striped tape around his ears and lips and mouth and hair. He was allowed to continue seeing. The father's eyes stayed focused on the room from every angle as they logrolled him out the door. Through the vehicle's back window, the father saw something draped across the house.

DEEP FOCUS

Upstairs the mother stood in the shower with her clothes on. Wet had collected in the room up to her knees and she was singing. Through the bathroom window, on her tiptoes, the mother saw the men corral the father into the car. The mother sang louder, closed her eyes. With soap the mother lathered a bearded mask around her head. In the sheen of many bubbles there were ballrooms, there were halls.

BODY

The mother came into the son's room with her hair up in a towel. The towel was made of other hair. The mother did not know where the hair had come from. She'd found many other things made of hair: afghans, hats, rugs, carpet, confetti, wigs, transistors—homes for bugs. The towel was soft and warming and seemed to suck the mother's skull.

The son was in the bed asleep, several blankets piled on top. So many blankets. The mother wondered how he could breathe through all that cotton—or all that silk or polyester or maybe hair, whatever. In the middle of the son's floor the carpet was all stained and rusty, gunked and bright with oxidation. The mother walked across the stain and felt her brain take light in photocopied. She stopped.

She moved toward the bed. The mother stopped and moved toward the bed again. The mother stopped and moved toward the bed. She looked and found she was further from the

bed than when she'd started. She could see how far the bed was and reached to touch it. The bed was right in front of her. She kneeled into the bed and felt her back bend. She had on so much blush and rouge and lipstick the son might not recognize her if he could see. She wanted him to see a little. She pulled the covers back off of the son's head. The son's eyes were open, glassed. He did not answer the mother's question but he was breathing fine, okay. Deep sleep. Deep sun. The son's breath smelled of old flowers. The mother covered up the son.

OH

In her own room again the mother touched herself with her best fingers, rubbing skin to skin against her gut, the house inside her egg-shaped belly—night above her—a silence made of towns. Each time she came she blacked out and when she came back she began again in mimicked moan.

PLEASE RESPOND

1. *The son was in the house.*

    Q: HOW MANY CURTAINS DID THE HOUSE HAVE?

    A:

    Q: DID THE HOUSE WANT THE SON IN IT?

    A:

    Q: WAS THE SON IN THE HOUSE?

    A:

2. *The son slept for several months—though in this state, via several internal forces i.e. wanting i.e. loss—time refracted through the son's body and therefore within the house it passed as only seven hours.*

Q: IF SOMEONE WERE STANDING NEAR OR AT OR IN THE SON'S BODY, OTHER OUTSIDE FORCES NOTWITHSTANDING, HOW MANY TOTAL MONTHS OR HOURS WOULD THAT PERSON AGE?

A:

Q: HOW LONG DOES IT TAKE NEW FLESH TO WRINKLE?

A:

Q: I FEEL VERY OLD AND TIRED.

A:

3. *One year earlier the son had discovered a small panel in the floor under his bed—a panel that, when opened, revealed a narrow passage down which the son could reach his hand. The son reached and reached and felt something down there nudge his knuckles. When the son removed his hand he found a short brass penny nail had been stuck into the loose skin between his thumb and pointer finger. The son took the nail out and looked at it and touched it to his tongue. The son swallowed the penny nail.*

Q: IS THE SON STUPID?

A:

Q: HOW ELSE COULD THE NAIL HAVE BEEN USED?

A:

Q: HOW MUCH DID THE SON BLEED?

A:

4. *In the son's sleep, the son was sleeping. In the sleeping sleep, the son had a dream. In the dream the son knew as given that the son would never die.*

Q: HOW MANY OTHER SONS WERE IN THIS DREAM? SONS THE SON COULD NOT SEE. SONS HIDING IN THE SLEEP WALLS. WHO ELSE'S SONS?

A:

Q: IS THAT TRUE? WOULD HE NOT EVER DIE?

A:

Q: WHY COULD NOT THE SON JUST SLEEP AND SLEEP?

A:

UNGIFT

The son's cell phone rang nonstop blitzed no pausing. On vibrate, the phone would shake so hard it shook the bed, the air. The vibration continued even when the son turned the phone off.

The son did not want to look at the phone's face to see who was calling in this way.

The son did not want to look. His eyes above, below, and beside him.

The son took the phone into the bathroom and hid the phone inside the drawer.

From the bedroom he could hear the porcelain of the sink above the drawer cracking under strain. He could hear the mirror patter. He could hear the soap dish dance. Something warped the bevel of the walls.

The son sat as long as he could manage on the corner of his bed, trying not to think. The bed was pushing up beneath him.

The son did not want not to touch the phone but the house would not be quiet. He went and got the phone where the bathroom was now raining dust. There were hundreds of him even in that mirror.

He went and lay down on the mattress with the phone against his chest.

The son felt sick again.

The son tried to call the mother's name but he heard his voice stay hung inside him, gushing in his gush.

MASSIVE FABRIC

The mother stood on the back lawn. The grass grew to her waist. She had her wet arms up over her head. Something flat above her—something there—she could almost touch it— could almost pull it down. A kind of skin or greasy fabric. Gash. A veil. She kept reaching. Her arm muscles began to stretch weird. Each time she brought her hands back down from reaching she felt her elbows bobbed a little further out. Bowed. Redistracted. Her pupils spacing outward, going lazy. She was so big now. She couldn't keep her hands from making knots. She couldn't keep her knees between her legs. The thing—perhaps an awning—was flattening the house.

Like the mother's body, the house all seemed to sag. The roof slid sloppy. The doors expanding. In countless windows the glass reflected the grass and gravel back onto the yard. A dead horse appeared in some parts of the reflection, its horseflesh buzzered and warped to gleaming waves from nonexistent heat. The mother's mother crouched down on the

horse's back, holding the egg against her chest. The egg glowed, singeing the night. The mother shouted at the mother's image, seething—all those years and years buried between—the mother's mother having made the mother and then left her in the air of every day, such silence—the new flesh they had made, in passing on.

From the mother's throat, instead of voice now, up through her chest there came a key— another key that opened nothing—*smooth teeth*—each further word a key and key again, their metal raining from her mouth in exclamation to click against the ground—and in turn to turn to further birds there, bursting, one and another, a white excrement, alive— each bird flying right after the other straight up and head-on into the thickening awning of the sky.

The mother shouted at the awning, keys erupting, uncounted birds in muscled shriek. She needed to pull the awning down, she knew, and knew she knew she would not. The stink of skin coursed new all through the air just beneath the edge of air where the long sky grew, growing hair, a body, trust.

Among the birds, the mother screamed another name. Her nostrils made little rooms for sluicing, her throat skin rawing into blood. Her skin pocked with insects that poured out from her brain, born from other, tiny eggs. There were gnats and ants and bees and beetles. There were flies of every color. These too flew to become something—of the awning, and the ground. The mother could not count herself, the shake inside her. More insects settled on the air—insects both from her and in the world compiling. They made it hard to blink, or want. Each little tic of need and knowing begged so much thought. The mother—she could not—hardly—inhale—she could not—see. She pulled her outermost clothes up over around her head, a mask. She breathed into the scummy cloth. The mother reached for names she'd heard there, those women and those men. The mother reached.

INITIATE

The son heard the hall door open and saw someone standing in the hall. This time the son did not hide or close his eyes, though he could not see through them quite clearly. The room was fuzzed. The son's arms were flexed as if for lifting. The figure in the hall stood unmoving for a long while. The son and the figure saw each other. The air around them seemed so empty it had no space. The son began to cough. The son could not move his head or hands and so instead hacked with his head back on the mattress, blooming germ-rind up above him. The son felt something metal in his mouth. The son coughed and coughed and spat a key. The key fell into the divot of his neck above the cell phone. The son's chest began to twitch. The key was sinking. The son saw the figure had come forward slightly. He saw the figure had a gown—or not a gown but some large curtain—or not a curtain but a cape—or not a cape but something muddy, something thin and flat and woven. The son felt the ants burrowed inside him skitter through his lungs dry like a hive.

The window light swung through quick cycles as the son watched the form emerge. The light and dark of sun and absence swam back and forth accelerated. The lip of light moved up the wall in shafts like blinkers, exposing the crudded sections where the son had hung the crud of his achievements. Among the light the form moved closer. It came in inches. It made no sound. The son could still not see. Even as the wash of light moved across the form, the son could not make out anything about it. The form's features were blurred or runny. The son blinked and blinked his eyes.

Sometimes between sets of blinking the son saw in the form's place an upright furry rabbit—a very young girl—an older man in a ratty yellow shirt, so hunched he could not stand. The son saw older versions of himself—much older, already balding, multi-tattooed from head to foot, carrying a book. Each of these ideas, though, remained replaced by the progressing form each time the son would blink. The son could not keep his eyes apart from one another. The son could not feel his feet.

O

Over time the figure proceeded and the son began to learn the figure's face. He could see the face and sensed a squirm a scrunch a need for recognition. Someone certain. Someone nearby. Someone the son had learned to love, though in a distant, ingrained method. The son had seen this person every day. He knew the smell. He knew the inches of the fabric of the thing the figure carried forward and wore all draped around it. The fabric was made of meat and blood and things undone and hair and years and wanting and a special blend of polyester. The son knew the figure's name inside him. The son felt something welling through his skin.

The cell phone was ringing so hard through the son now that he could feel the impending conversation. He could hear what the person on the other end would be saying and he could hear his voice reply. He'd heard those words a billion times too. He heard them every time he slept. He said them in dreams of people he did not know yet. He said them in very

tiny rooms. He spoke them out into the bedroom also. The bedroom's walls had absorbed so much. The son wanted to touch the bedroom walls again. The son wanted to stand up. The son's skin was getting ugly. A bubble flooded on his neck. He popped the bubble with his finger. Another rose. He popped and popped. He could feel the hemming of his lines, becoming sizes. He could feel his last haircut aching in the tendrils of the hair he sometimes—like the father—devoured in his sleep. In his sleep the son had eaten more than anyone could ever. There was so much in the son. The son could kill a forest if he shaved. The son could cripple nations. The son could sew designer jeans out of his runoff.

Everything.

The son could hear the prior homeowners's pets, which were endlessly buried in the backyard and underneath the house and sometimes even under the gravel of the driveway or in the carpet underneath the son's bed.

The son's skin was coming off.

The figure stood closer. The fabric the figure had unfolded stunk and filled the room. More beef. A little cream. Graham crackers. The son loved graham crackers—he liked the crack between teeth—he'd eaten enough to build a mall—the figure knew this. The figure had a mouth, the son could see that, he could see inside the mouth. The son could see the room flooding with liquid. The son could see the apartment the figure rented in the figure's chest.

The son could not laugh either, but he did too.

The room was getting warmer—sweating. The son's posters slipped off the walls. The ink slid from off the posters and the paint from off the place where they had hung. The paint

coagulated into pigments. The son felt a blister open on his top lip. He had a suntan. He had a sunburn. Months of sunburns. Years in years. Sun damage. Damage. He grew thicker.

The figure was off the width of a fist now, give or take a hair. The son had made many fists but wanted to make more. Once the son had seen an ocean slip out of the crack slit in the windshield of a car, a car cracked as the son watched and made the car skid with his eyes. The son's hair contained the cells of everyone he'd ever been.

Actually, the son could laugh a little, though it came out through his back and sunk into the bed. The son was sneezing colors. The son had lanterns in his eyes—lanterns once used to light other houses. The son felt someone sewing his perimeter into the clothgrain of the bed. He blinked and found himself inside a mattress on top of which someone was sitting—someone asleep or still or reading or too tired to stand up—someone maybe thinking of the son—maybe the son himself. The son saw days he'd spent already layered across the room in film. The son watched his head in photo portraits his mother had made him hang up on his room's walls wilt in time-lapse backward, his skin becoming puckered, regressing into cells. The son was inside the mother then and could see the mother's moving arms. The mother digging, bug-swarmed. The son could read the things the mother had not meant to think about the son—the thoughts pummeled through and through her—her imagination's doubt. The son saw the mother through the mother. Saw the mother lying on a bed. Saw the mother coursed with wrinkles, her coarse white hair. The mother in a very tiny room.

The son could not fully sit up. He felt his blood gush inside a spiral. He fell straight down through long darkness. His neck was getting tired.

The son.

The son felt older. He grew a mustache, faint at first and then a handlebar, one that, if he could move his hands, he would have twisted at the ends into a creation that would have made him memorable in pictures. The son's voice inside him changed—though he could not use it, he could hear several other sounds projected—other people.

Other people in the son.

The son grew capable of babies—capable of son. A billion sperm.

The son shed skin at a rate that made his body lift off the mattress inch by inch. The room was filling up. His fingernails were curling. His eyes changed color twice—once to gold like change he'd hidden—once to the shade of blue the summer sky had been the day the father and the mother had made the son on the very bed the son sprawled on now.

The son's back began to crimp. The son felt his hands go loose a little.

Above the bed the ceiling was bowing down. It bowed to touch the center of the moment where the son and the figure would collide. The walls as well had swum with hump, puckered funny, pulling out. Hair, skin, liquid, money. The carpet sat slathered in frustration, stapled to the ground.

O

The figure hung right there above the son. The figure had the longest hair. The figure's hair was lashed into the son's hair. They had the same hair. The hair grew shorter, pulling taut. The son looked into the figure. The figure was long in moments and scratched in others. The figure has someone else inside it also. Populations. Masses. Burning. The figure wore the son's original shade of pupils, refracted now with shards of foreign color—red—red like the son's bruises, like bricks for houses or wall paint, red the color the son had shat the week he ate all the mother's lipstick, the mother's lipstick in him, red like certain birds not yet exploded for the air, red like the son inside the son and the son the son could have had himself.

The son and the figure were mouth to mouth. Their lips were cracked and puffy. They breathed back and forth to one another. Their breath was made of the same cells. They breathed. They breathed. In each breath there was another word, and in each word there was another, and the son began to see the things the son would never see. They breathed.

DAYS

The massive vehicle slid along the street until it stopped in the new rut around the house. Something had sawed into the yard's perimeter, made a little ditch that ran with sludge and seemed to sink into itself. The vehicle's soundless transmission warped several birds out of the sky, raining the birds onto the windshield, their carcasses then sucked into a suction and used to fuel the vehicle. The back window of the vehicle folded down and out of it pushed the father.

The father rolled down along the back hood and off the bumper into the street. He bruised his elbows on the pavement, bleeding clear. He stood up shaking and watched the long white vehicle drive off. The vehicle bruised the ground.

The father was naked except for a metal bulb around his head. Two tiny slits allowed him to see out. There were not slits for ears or nose or mouth. The father had gained weight. The

men had fed the father through long weird tubes and turkey basters. He did not know how long he'd been gone. There were no official charges. He'd been fully reprimanded. He'd been made to solve crossword puzzles in a small translucent box at the bottom of a public swimming pool, through which in his mind he could see the chubby men and women in their slick suits holding their children while they peed. He could see all the stuff the people's bodies flushed into the water, which came and stuck to the perimeter of the father's box. The crossword puzzles were designed to trigger complicated extrasensory properties. The father filled in 49 ACROSS with the word *LASAGNA* and could taste it in his mouth. That was the good part. The father had had to fill in many other less delightful words—such as *LESION*, such as *NEED*, such as—such as—such as . . .

Many other things, like all things, the father could not remember.

He could not remember losing skin.

He could not remember the skull-sized beams of other light they'd shined into his forehead and in the ruts behind his knees, *resetting the deletion, blank of blank on blank*. All the foot-long pins they'd used, and the sledgehammer, and the prism and the dice. Days extracted in blood pictures. Doorbells. Birthdays. His new name(s). He could not remember anything about the other house, the box.

The father could not remember, in any form, the son—the grain of skin or glint of eye the child had in those first hours, as if having been rubbed with steel wool in the womb; the thin months thereafter in which he could still hold the child in a warm silence against his father chest, pleasant, grinning, before the son had learned to scream; the smell ejected from the holes that kicked out his baby teeth, like wire and old cheese—*this smell had soon become so general it disappeared*. He could not remember the way for months at first, as the

child had begun speaking, he'd called the father by his full name, first, middle, and last; how some days, all days, the son walked backward, even his first steps, before the steps the father and the mother would witness as his "first," *the father had not known this ever anyway, at all*; or the letter the child had written to the father their fifth Christmas to say how much he loved the father, the letters out of order and poorly drawn, and the picture of the family there without faces, except the blackened O hole of the son's mouth at the exact center of his head, scribbled to rip. He did not remember the son's want and wishing, his decorations, their hours before the house while suns would rise, buses arriving to take the son off to some far location, the father on the lawn then waiting for his return in a light; evenings, hours, suppers, cushions, floors; invented games, the blanket mazes, puzzles. How the son could hide for hours in the house and not be found. The father no longer, in his body, held to an inch of this. He could not, in any alley of his remaining mind there, of what the men had left, recall a single thing about the child that stuck inside him but as bumping, but as tremor, itch, or slur. The exit colors beating underneath his forehead, the window of his lungs.

THE REPEATING NIGHT

The father moved to stand in what remained of his only home's cracked driveway, holding his head up with his hands. The bulb was very heavy. Inside the bulb it smelled like meat. Outside the bulb it smelled like meat. All air was meat now, as was water. The meat was see-through, at least, thank god. All on the air the bugs were crawling—the caterpillars, the ants, the geese. Most geese aren't bugs but these were. The paint on this side of the house had now shifted in its tone. It'd grown to match the grass that'd grown almost above the father's head. On the roof there was an enormous blanket half-tied down. It looked like the baby blanket the son had slept with for years and years until they'd had to take it away for quarantine. Massive cameras hung in the ozone, aimed directly at the house, spooling film down on the planet, long black translucent ticker tape splayed like raining.

In the sky above the house it looked like any other day.
Outside the house the grass was growing. The sun was smuggy. The street was gone. The

neighbors did not mend their houses from recent damage. There was too much on the news. Several shopping malls went bust. An ocean liner ate its own weight. The library of the son's school filled up with dust, though only in the evenings, so no one could know. A theme park became a peach and had a bite eaten in it where kids fell in and drowned. In the sky above the house there was a smoking but it was also clear, and it also smelled like endless beef and yet dogs stayed hidden, cowered. A moving van grew fat with girls. There were other people in their own windows, though they did not know what they were looking for. Gun shops did their business and did it well. Several popular websites were replaced with blocks of color. The grocery stores did not have eggs though they paid their men to stock them. The druggists were on drugs. Something had chewed on the largest building in the downtown district. Populations sweltered. The text in all the books in all bookstores increased in size by millimeters. You could not take a bath. The magicians were disappearing and not coming back to smile and swing their arms to end the show. Stores opened in every strip mall selling only handsaws. Babies came out with pubic hair and tried to crawl back inside their mothers. Women were older much more often. Email servers learned to laugh. You could not press *Save* on your MS Word files, only *Save As* . . .—unto all things a new name. The ocean grew a tumor. The moon grew a tumor. The president grew a tumor and ate it on TV into a large microphone, making the sound of years to come. You couldn't sing or cry or chew or want or listen or know or sneeze. This all happened in one wrecked second. *Where were we then?*

The house remained the same.

The father trampled through the tall grass looking for a way to the front door. He could not quite aim himself toward the destination. The grass flapped at his hair. He could see the part of the house above the doorway where the night lamps glowed now a little bright. The father hacked and hacked the grass down with his sore limbs and walked and thought and looked and moved and walked and thought and thought and walked and looked and moved.

DOPPELGÄNGER MANTRA

Inside the bulb the father spoke.

He was repeating everything he'd ever said throughout his life now once again.

On a tiny panel in the bulb's interior, LCD nodules tallied each word, how many times.

The top ten words:

WHAT

NO

NOT

HELLO or HI

(*HIS NAME*)

PLEASE

SON

OUCH

OH

GOODBYE

The father's voice splashed off the metal, right back into his face.

HIVE

By the time the father found the front door it was locked. The naked father did not have his key. The men had kept it. The welcome mat was gone. Ants swarmed the stain on the concrete where it had been fed the residue. The naked father touched his flesh as if it might have hidden pockets—*and though it did he could not find them*. The father beat the door and rang the bell. The father browned his fists. Sometimes the buzzer shocked him. Sometimes the buzzer played Brahms, sometimes black metal, sometimes the soothing sound of rain-forest water or a shriek of someone being burned. These windows had been painted over or blocked off. The father put his eye up to the spy hole. Peering backward through it he felt a squirt. Inside the father's chest was also squirting. He pulled the knob until it came off. The knob cauterized his hand. There'd also been a key under the plant box, though its base had been cracked through. The soil spilled out and ants had ravaged that, eating innards out of the leaves and leaving strange veined wire. The plant's roots grew into the concrete so deep the father could not lift the box up. Some of the roots had little pods like eyes. So much movement—little sound.

As the father turned from the house, someone behind the door watched through the window.

The father loped back into the high grass, grown even higher since his arrival. The father fought to forge a path. He toppled forward with the bulb off-balance. The grass cut tons of tiny marks across his naked arms and legs and belly. The father's testicles were swollen. He had a limp in both his legs. The father's legs were now prosthetic, as were his chest and lungs and muscle—as was the vast majority of the father—though the father felt the same.

The father tottered through the growth with his head half at his knees. The bulb kept sweating. He could hear dogs around him packed in masses. He could hear a billion humming bees. All through the grass, hung on the blades around and on the house, the bugs were scumming up a hive. Countless interlocking pockets wet with bee grease, clasped in combs—each hole an eye—each eye a yawning. One long buzz. As well, in the soil below the swim of hive stuff, the ants were laying bed foundation—dirt clipped in piles and stacked as turrets, torrents, entry gaps large enough to suck around the father's foot. The father danced and leapt and rolled along and through the yard with welts already forming on his knees—pocks on his sternum—chiggers kissed inside his ankles. He felt dizzy with new data. His mouth began to foam. In the foam his words popped as bubbles. The LCD clicker ran up and up. With each curse word, use of god's name, or fault of grammar, the father received a cram of shock.

POPULATION

The father came into another clearing around the house's right side. The paint on the house here peeled in scores. The curled paint resembled larvae, and so that's what they were. There was a window looking in. The father moved to touch the window with cramping fingers. He clanged his metal forehead on the glass but it would not break. He clawed the glass and got some wedged under his nails.

Through the eyeslits the father could see somewhat—into the TV room, though there was no TV now, no other stuff. The TV room had not had a window on the inside, but from outside he could see in. The room contained ten to twenty people—on second thought, more like fifty or a hundred—on third, more like five hundred or ten thousand—teeming like ants, colliding, impossible to count. The father saw himself, the mother, and the son therein among the mingling, chewing cheese and crackers off tiny plates. Others also looked familiar. With each new head the father felt his recall swim for some connection.

The whole room overflowed. Keys and eggs and blood and money. Thinning wives and headless men. Young boys with rings and electronic money. The father saw the man and woman who'd appeared to buy the house and recognized them, though he had not been home when they'd come to see the house before, and he could not see how both of them resembled younger versions of himself and her, *whomever,* and here their heads were tied together by the hair—they had one set of hair between them. The whole house did. They were all speaking into cubes. Everyone with his or her head against a black box, skin growing fatter on their heads. A mush. You could see transmissions on the air—could read the baggage hanging on the slow slopes where all together we were breathing in and out. The rooms not rooms but years. Along the walls the new wallpapered shapes repeating: O.

O of *go* and *how* and *nowhere.*

O of *house* and *son* and *door.*

O of *O.*

From outside looking in, the father beeped and banged against the glass. No one would look toward him. They all were asking. Inside the house the boxes rang, and heads made laugh and bees barfed buzz and long dogs barked and babies babbled, while inside his bulb the father began to shout a semi-prayer and the bulb zapped his skin and skull in hot correction and across it all there was a wind and no one would.

COCOON GAZEBO

In the backyard, high as ever, like long blank curtains to the sky, the father swung and bit and bashed his head cutting a pathway in the green. His tongue had begun to gather in his helmet, dislodged somewhere way back down his throat, the weird mashed meat surround-compiling in the space around his cheeks. Likewise, his breath had begun building layers on the bulb's condensation-proof glass. The father tried to wink his cheek to rub the glass clean, but that was hard.

Somewhere in the yard among the fallen clothesline and loops of dead brown meat once trees, the father came to a gazebo nestled in the growing. A tall thin black corrupted structure, thick and pointed though dented in along the top as if something large had had nabs at it. The father did not like its sweeter smell, etched with the sickness, the surrounding air suffused with more mosquitoes, wasps—*had you seen this air here, you could not see*—the father tripped his way up beneath the errored awning and into the dark shell, buzzing, smoke.

The father knew that though he'd never seen it, the gazebo had always been in the yard, and always would be, in any yard. The father had had long dreams of coiling in a hammock, eating. Here. There were many things the father had planned to do—in or around the house or other—lists of lists of lists of lists—this gazebo, too, was those. The father walked into its mouth.

From up inside the structure's bleach-burnt stomach, the father could hear the mother somewhere shout. He could not make out what she said—her voice compiled of several others—a thousand tonalities at once—heads surrounding the gazebo, skin on skin, and air on air. The gazebo walls were screened completely and hung with new-car-scent plumes and bags of rice. A sheet of pupae blocked the holy wire scrim. They were crusted on so thick—*such dedication*—the gazebo's size quadrupled, like a crown.

The father could not stop with turning, turning, seeing the same few feet of textured surface, until he fell dizzy on the wood.

BAG

When he could think again, the father saw a long black bag hanging from the gazebo ceiling. Hung above by strands of hair, it had a name tag and numbers that the father could not read. The father sat up and reached to touch the bag. He felt it warming under his rub. He felt the wets and bumps and whorls. *Kick. Kick kick. Kick.* Somewhere the mother went on shouting. On certain words, the father's language tally meter would mistake her words for his. *Zap.*

BLANK

The father unzipped the bag. The metal teeth moaned. Inside the bag the father saw the son curled and snoozing, his hands folded at his face. The father felt a wash of whipping through his back, throat, and aorta. Hey, the father said. He could not recall the son's name. He tried a few. The current scourged him. The hair grew on his face.

EITHER

The father shook the son unknowing until he opened up his eyes. From in the bag, the son glared. The father could hardly see the son through the glass inside the helmet, for all his sound and all the hair, the rip. What, the son kept repeating, eyes closed, screaming. What. What. What. What. What. What. Each *what* flew upward from him toward some nothing that on other days he'd called a sky. The son's sound against the helmet made the father's language tallies reset to zero, zero, zero. The father, fried.

COPY OF A COPY OF A COPY

Through a window in the house
that looked out onto the backyard
the son watched the buzzing father
rouse himself (the son). The son felt
amused. He fixed his hair in the re-
flection. He tried to speak but made
a mess.

And then the son was outside the
house there with the father and the

father's arms were wet and kind of
mushy and the son tried to sit up
and felt something hold him and
felt something moving through his
lungs, new words wanting out and
worming, clustered in his bulb. The
father could not see the bulb was
see-through, made of days.

And then the son was in the house
again looking out and the air was fully
solid and the son stood encased inside
the air and through the window there
was light.

LIGHT OF YEARS LIGHT OF WINDOWS LIGHT OF GROWING LIGHT OF NEED

And then the son stood at the kitchen
table eating waffles watching TV
laughing, sneezing, and all the pres-
sure in his knees, and there were all
these people all around him and they
were pushing up against his back,
they cawed, and they knocked the
table to the left and right and they
lifted the table off the ground, and
the light inside the drink inside the
son's stomach from the girl's house
began to chew into his chest, and he
laughed harder, and everyone was

laughing too, all around him bodies
laughing, and his teeth began to turn
inside his head and he could not see
and he could not remember and he
was so hungry the ceiling wobbled
up and down.

And then the son was being carried
through the massive lawn with all
the mud splashing up around them,
and the sky or ceiling stretching
overhead and coming closer down
and closer down, and the son could
feel his cheeks all puffy and the son
could feel his and his father's heart-
beats both together through his own
chest, the visor of the father's helmet
banging back and forth against the
son's skull's hardened soft spot in the
rhythm of their fumbling run.

And then the son was in the son's room looking at all the clear gel spilling from the closet, the closet where the son had spent so many hours typing still unknown, and the son saw what he made, he saw the texture of the ejection, of the words burped from several selves he'd held in hives, layers wished and crushed and in him, and he felt the words spread through the room expanding, felt the words burst back into him and through and through and of the room, words worn on paper, wet and endless, a flooding ocean at his knees, at his chest, his neck, his head, gel gumming up his nostrils and in the air vents, in the air itself—and then the son again could not breathe—and the words slushed and slammed around the son as massive slivers, blubbing up, and the son rose off the floor inside the rising, and the son tried to swim and kick as best he could, the language welling in his head and stomach, stretching his legs and muscles, and therein the

son gushed on, and the son slid down
through the hallway, wide as ever,
and the son warbled down the stairs,
down through the house where all
was runny and one color, and the son
gushed on through the front door—

and then the son opened his mouth and shut
his eyes and then the son slid backward through where he'd
been and the son saw seas and rooms and constellations and the
son grew very large and he grew small—

and then the son was in the father's arms gel-covered, and the son was the father's
arms themselves and they were standing there beside the mother at a hole large as the
house, a hole with many holes inside it, *concentric rings of endless holes inside the hole*, and
the mother's head was wound with bees and birds and gel and she had a shovel and she was
digging in the rip, and she was digging and she was digging, begging in the holes—she was
saying something about the father or the son or both together, and the mother ripped and
bent her long nails on the hard dirt—the dirt that had built up around the house high as
the house and ever higher at the hole's edge and yet had not yet found a way to touch the

sky—and the father tried to make the mother put the shovel down and come away from the half-assed hole she'd hardly dug inside the hole, among all the other holes there all around her, and she there screaming on and on into the grass about insects and sand and windows and the houses and the light—

and her warm body—

and her rubbed insides—

and all her wanting, measured in flume—

and all the rooms she'd never seen, and the rooms those other rooms contained—

and her need for forgiveness—

and her life—

and then the mother turned and turned, around in nothing,
swinging the shovel at the father—

and the yard was smushed around them burned and buzzing—and the sky was smacked

and stretched with mold and slip—and the trees were splotched with sores and raining

color— and the son could not see the father could not see the mother could not see—

—from above the house—and around the house—despite these things—the house could not be seen—the house was hidden, sat in dry air cold and throat-choked with vast collision, all minor manner of humming creature swarmed in spirals through the sound—a sound of something soaked and squashed stung forever in the house's lining—beneath the roof all bulged and scumming over through the thicket of new trees—bees and bats and ants and crows and cranes and gulls and geese and ducks and dogs and helicopters and doves and pigeons, dragonflies, gnats hung on waves from towers gashed in the weird glow of the sky's head with translucent stepladders which in the warble now descended, folding and unfolding, cradled around the house, surrounded—this house with no good door—this house in which the son sat—the house in which other families had also sat and still were sitting, through which bodies had moved and opened doors and breathed the air and fucked and gone to sleep—the son with his head a box of years he'd had and years still yet impending—the son's vibrating mucous membranes—the son's serrated eyes—the son

with his head rubbed quite wide open in the house slicked cream-thick from eave to eave—
the rats and ruts and burns corroded—the sky above it wet with need, the sky colliding,
the sky unfolded, the sky reflecting back itself—the son above the bed now levitating or
coiled to nothing or not quite there—the windows of the swarmed house bending over
curling in, falling out a final time to allow the entrance of things banging, begging—their
heads a hammer—the house's floors and carpets slathered, layer after layer, sight unseen—
the house's windows glossing over, revealing things that had been there and yet were not,
not even now, yet, things etched on the breath hung as remainder—some reminder, who
and who and who, what beds these rooms had nuzzled, what walls the brighter air had
seemed—the son unraveled—the son's cracked back—the globes of light creased and com-
piling—slurring junk sloughed off, ejected—the light wires crimped and full of glisten
and new need—the house's spreading open—the rooms revealing all in one moment what
they'd been and seen and shown—what they wanted—who else they were once, what other
inches, who they could be anew again—and the son's lips and lids and other eyes and pores
and holes and follicles sang fat with foam—the son congealing—the son in every window
of the house—the son the size of the house, inside—the house walls swelling, the weird
unbuckle, the teeming crust riddled with creak, the living layer they'd created warping—
gel—the buzz of black transmission—the other houses—the tattoo ratted over the father's
eyes, the son's, though the mother could almost peek, the mother who'd slipped this riddle,
hole of holes there, the mother half inside the son—he in her and she in he and they in
ever—the mother could feel the other weight, she could feel him lifted upward—the house
now big as some balloon, the old walls warped and cragged with yawn or screeching—the
house deforming—all other houses—homes—the sky a soft black zero as the son b u l g e d
o u t t h r o u g h t h es o u n d—

SOUND OF TRUMPETS SOUND OF SIGHING SOUND OF SHOTGUNS SOUND OF
GEESE SOUND OF GLIMMER SOUND OF NOWHERE SOUND OF SON

—and in the midst of all of this, from the outside, from neighbor's doors or windows and in the street—from all but a certain very minor other angle there was no way for most to see what had gone on—you could not see that this wasn't one of many houses—from the street the house was fine— A-OK—today, tomorrow—on the walk the neighbors passed in silent indecision—*what for dinner? glass or chicken?*—though in the minute on the hour their skin went prickled near their teeth, they looked a second time in one direction, pulled their pets along to shit on somewhere else—that night they didn't kiss their sons or wives— they grew one more new long hair or felt a ticker in their thigh—only in their sleep then could they see what they had seen.

HALLWAY

The son was in the bedroom.

The son was standing on the bed. He'd brought the mirror back out from the closet and unsheathed it. The son felt very tired. The son shrunk and expanded both at once—so that from the outside the son seemed to stay the same size.

The mirror had fingerprints and footprints and breath steamed on the glass from, it seemed, several sides.

The son stood above the mirror. The son saw the mirror from above. With the masked light flooding through the room's enormous window—a light that flickered, flexed and charred—the light of so many different days—the mirror seemed to bend. With his head like this and arms like this and humming, the son could see a hallway in the glass. And then

depending on what the son wished or how he wanted or remembered or forgot—the son could make the hallway open up. The son could make the hallway fold around him.

The son could slip into the hall.

The son walked down the hall with both eyes blinking in and out and in and out.

The son walked and walked and walked. The son felt lighter. The son's arms began to shake.

The son came to a door.

The light continued. Light ate light up, and shat light out, and light remained. Days rolled in the long blows of the hours hidden in spinning years and months and days.

In the houses men were laughing. Mothers made other mothers, fathers, too. Sick continued. Night continued. In the night, small pockets fried in endless sing.

The night gathered up in pockets, grew holes. The holes hummed around a rasping center, rolled. Centered in all air and in all bodies. The center's center had no name.

The bodies aged. The bodies ate lunch, their old limbs shifting, breathing up in celebration, years of air. Resting. Nesting. Needing. Sleeping. Going. Sewing. Teeth on teeth.

Other things would happen. More words would pass from mouth to mouth. The weight of nameless light would overflow the houses, days unblinking, above ground.

The ground was light. The lunch was light, too. And the days, the beds, more holes. The light would fill the halls for hours. The skin would come and come and come.

ACKNOWLEDGMENTS

Thank you, Calvert Morgan, magicmachine. Thank you, Carrie Kania, Dennis Cooper, Bill Clegg. Thank you, mother, father, sister, brother-in-law. Thank you, Heather. Thank you, Gene & *HTMLGiant* crew. Thank you, *Featherproof* crew. Thank you, Ken, Shane, Gian, Michael, David, Sean, Derek. Thank you, Atlanta friends. Thank you, Internet. Thank you.